The Cardinal
& the Hawk

Alice Kanaka

This book is a work of fiction. The events and characters portrayed are imaginary. Their resemblance, if any, to real-life counterparts is entirely coincidental. Actual places are used in a fictional context and this story is in no way portraying any real events, staff, internal workings, or management.

Table of Contents

<u>**Other Books by Alice Kanaka**</u>

The Cardinal & The Crow
The Cardinal, The Fat Boy, & The Flamingo

<u>**Coming Soon**</u>

Bumfuzzle and Cattywampus: Unlikely Detectives
Trouble at the Buckeye Festival

Chapter 1

Sam crouched behind a tree as another arrow whizzed over her head. Blood seeped through her jacket where the first had grazed her arm. Adrenaline pounded through her system; the pain and cold were secondary to survival. Although she was sweating, she dared not remove her white snowsuit's hood; her bright red hair against the snow-covered landscape would serve as a perfect target.

Tom attempted to cross the clearing below. One moment he was walking; the next, he was falling forward with an arrow protruding from his large rucksack. Sam's throat tightened, and bile threatened as he fell. Her first instinct was to run to him, but a large arm grabbed her from behind, and a gloved hand covered her mouth before she could scream. Panic set in, taking over any lucid thought. She threw her head back, but her attacker was tall, and her head glanced off his shoulder. Quickly bending and reaching through her legs to grab his knee, he dodged her attempt. She tried to yank his fingers apart, grabbed for his ear, nothing worked. As a last resort, she was prepared to pull her .28 out of her boot when her assailant whispered, "You can't save him if you're dead."

Sam suddenly stopped fighting and slumped against him. Her heartbeat was painful in her chest, and she put her hand over it as she struggled to slow her breathing. "Are you trying to give me a heart attack?"

"I didn't know how else to stop you. You were primed to sprint." Art let go, and she turned to look at him. "Set off your flare."

Sam pulled it out of her pack with shaky hands and discharged it into the sky above the clearing.

"I'm going down to head off the shooters. Cover me and whoever comes to help Tom."

"I'm afraid, Art. Who are they?"

"You're strong. It will be okay." He gave her a fist bump and headed down through the wooded perimeter without answering her question.

Observing his descent, Sam was amazed as always by how lithe and quiet he could be. He was an incredible instructor, the most knowledgeable survivalist she had ever met, and he was built like a bear.

Sam stayed very still, rifle drawn, scanning the clearing and the trail as Art descended. Three figures and a dog approached Tom from the direction of her camp. She recognized Roger, her head ranch hand, and his Australian Shepherd immediately. The snowsuits made recognition more challenging, but Roger had the distinctive gait of a cowboy, and Ben, their chef, was recognizable because of his size. *The other person must be one of the campers.*

When the three men reached Tom, they dove into the snow as an arrow flew toward the clearing. Sam lowered her rifle and shot into the woods on her right. *Where's Art? He isn't shooting arrows.* Roger looked up and seemed to look right at her but stayed with Tom. Sam covered them until they had returned to the relative safety of the woods below the clearing. *Please let Tom be okay. I can't lose him now.*

After they had gone, she turned her attention to the path Art had taken. She heard the rustle of branches and thought she saw a flash of brown fabric. Birds stilled, and low branches swayed subtly, approaching her position. It wasn't Art; she wouldn't have heard him. She ducked again, pulse racing. Throwing a rock to her right and receiving an arrow in return, she shot her rifle in the archer's direction and sprinted farther uphill.

Sam's snowshoes were designed for running, and she practiced with them daily. Her long legs propelled her across the snow with surprising speed. Very familiar with the forest and armed, she could easily outrun her pursuer, who would likely proceed with caution. Her adrenaline kept her going for a while, as she zigzagged through the trees, but the heavy rucksack she carried, and the deep snow caused her lungs and her legs to burn. Her resting periods became closer and closer together until she was stopping every fifteen minutes, scanning her environment, and listening intently.

The woods had a life of their own, and she jumped every time she heard a branch crack or bushes rustle. The shooter never appeared. Sam finally reached a small, rocky creek and headed upstream several hundred feet before leaving the creek bed and covering her tracks with a pine branch. *By morning there will be no trace.*

Sitting behind an outcrop of boulders, Sam drank some water and rested briefly. This was not what she envisioned when she carefully planned the opening week of her survival school. *I wonder where Art is. I hope he's okay. Does he know who the shooter is?* The archer had aimed at her before Tom entered the scene. She knew she was the target but had no idea why. *Does it have something to do with Art?*

Traveling uphill and slightly to the east, Sam searched for the densest tree cover she could find. Settling for a thicket among a circle of ancient pines, she pulled out her entrenchment-tool and began to clear the snow beneath an enormous tree. Although exhausted, her arm throbbing, she knew she would freeze without shelter.

Once she had cleared a sufficiently capacious area, she pulled out her knife and hunted for smaller saplings she could use for support beams. The muscles in her hands and arms screamed as she slowly cut through the wood. *I wish I had a saw. This would be much easier with the proper tools.* She stopped numerous times to listen, worried she was making excessive noise, but as the shadows lengthened and the shooter didn't appear, she concluded that he had either abandoned the chase for the day or gone in the wrong direction.

Having cut down three saplings and shaved off their boughs, she used their trunks for support beams, lodging them against the side of the large pine tree in a triangular pattern. She tested their strength, then stacked the boughs, overlapping them to make her shelter. She worked hastily, to complete the shelter before dusk. The intense black of night would be daunting without a flashlight. Her mind worked as swiftly as her body, trying to comprehend why someone would want her dead.

Sam sat in her makeshift home and removed her heavy, down jacket and a thermal shirt. She shivered violently as she inspected her left arm. It was bloody and throbbing but only grazed. Carefully wiping the wound, she applied antibiotic ointment and gauze, then wrapped it well. By the time she was done, she was thoroughly chilled and grateful for her torn jacket. Using duct tape to patch the holes, she pondered her next steps. Although tempted to loop back for the extra rucksack her friends had left for her, the sun was setting, and she was already freezing. The distance she covered during the day would take much longer at night, so she opted to pile more boughs in her shelter, eat a protein bar, and settle in for the night.

Roger saw the flare go up. He headed out with his dog and two other campers to find whoever set it off. When they reached the clearing, he glimpsed a body lying in the snow, off in the distance, a dark outline on a wide expanse of gleaming snow. Roger's dog, Red, went bounding toward the prone figure, but Roger stopped and scanned the tree line before cautiously signaling for Ben and Scott to follow. As they got closer, Ben said, "Is that Tom?" He was a large man with a booming voice, but his stage whisper gave away his sense of danger. They began moving more urgently, as rapidly as they could in the deep snow.

When they got to him, Roger said, "Tom?" He released his bated breath as Tom groaned, then said, "Get down."

They dropped as an arrow whizzed by, then a gunshot rang out. Roger scanned the woods above them and saw someone in white aiming into the woods to their left.

Another shot rang out.

"I think Sam's covering us. Can you move, Tom?"

"Possibly, with some assistance. Something's wrong with my back."

"The arrow protruding from your pack appears a likely culprit."

Tom groaned. "Did it penetrate my back, or is it just jabbing me?"

Roger tried to lift the pack, but Tom stopped him. "Maybe you can just squeeze a sweater or something between me and the backpack, so it doesn't bounce."

"I think we should pull it out."

Roger gaped at Scott. *What an idiot. You really are high most of the time, aren't you?* "We'll talk about that back at camp." They began to rise as another shot rang out. Roger scanned the tree line again. "Let's make a run for it."

"More like a crawl for it," Tom moaned.

They weren't moving very quickly, but they made it out of the clearing. "Where's Sam?" Tom asked through clenched teeth.

"She's up in the tree line. I left my pack for her; in case she needs it."

"We have to go back for her."

"I don't know what's going on, but she's the only reason we were able to get you out of the clearing."

The distance back to camp was not more than a quarter of a mile, but their journey was painstakingly slow. Tom had to be supported on two sides and still wore his heavy pack. He became slower and weaker as they trudged through the deep snow. Roger's relief was palpable when he spied the outlines of the hot tents and the smoke rising through the stove pipes.

When they entered the first tent, Roger carefully raised the heavy pack to see if the arrow had gone through. The tip had penetrated

Tom's back but hadn't passed the barbs. A petite young woman with wispy, light brown hair rushed forward with concern. "What happened?"

Removing his snowsuit, Roger said, "Tom's been hit with an arrow. Do you have any herbs that can help with pain and fight infection until we can get help?"

"Yes." Melissa began digging through her bag of herbal remedies. "I have bromelain for pain. White willow bark might work better, but it causes blood thinning, so probably not good in this case." She rummaged some more. "I can use honey to protect the wound and prevent infection. Sam told me Jack was going to try to make it. He can help if he shows, and maybe his ride can either transport Tom or send for help."

Roger nodded, then turned his attention back to Tom. "Okay, Tom, we're going to get the arrow out, then let Melissa work her magic."

Melissa gripped Roger's shoulder. "Do you have any whiskey?"

Why would she ask me that?

"It might numb the area, so it doesn't hurt so much."

"You could give me an internal shot of that too." Tom chuckled and groaned.

"Internal first. It's going to hurt when it hits the wound."

"I might need a shot, too," Roger said, eyeing the arrow.

Whiskey dispensed, Ben held the pack's weight while Roger removed the arrow's tip, then slid the straps off Tom's shoulders. Ben quickly peeled off Tom's snowsuit, and Melissa tried to stanch the bleeding before helping him onto the cot.

"You were lucky, Tom. The arrow hit something in your pack that bent it and slowed it down. Otherwise, it would have gone right into your spine."

"Sam would say God was looking out for me. I hope he's taking care of her too." He laid down as instructed and grimaced as Melissa patched up his wound the best she could.

"See if you can get comfortable," she said.

Roger paced with his arms crossed. "Thanks, Melissa. Can you keep an eye on him? Don't let anyone else touch him?"

She tilted her head.

"Someone shot him. Someone else thought we should just pull the arrow out." He glanced in Scott's direction. "We need to make sure he's safe. I'll take turns with you through the night." Roger turned and motioned to Ben, who had been stripping off his snowsuit. "Both of you, keep an eye on the others tomorrow. Try to keep everyone together and make a note if anyone leaves. I'm going to search for Sam and don't want to worry about being shot while I'm out."

They both nodded and helped Roger fill a backpack with things he might need when he found her.

"Look after Red for me, Ben."

"I will. He and I are pals." Ben ruffled the fur on Red's head, and Red wagged his tail.

Roger smiled. "He knows a good food source when he sees one."

Chapter 2

Resting on her bed of boughs in an emergency reflective bag that helped her stay warm, Sam thought about Tom and her friends back at camp. *I wonder if Jack made it. Is Tom okay? I wish he was here with me. Are the campers nervous? Where is Art?* She thought of Tom. He had finally moved to Santo Milagro a few weeks previously, and they had settled into a comfortable routine at her ranch. Sam frowned. *Some honeymoon. We're both injured, and we aren't even together.* She drifted off toward dawn, picturing Tom's dancing blue eyes as they were at their Christmas wedding.

When the sun finally began its ascent, Sam opened her eyes and endeavored to organize her snarled thoughts. She couldn't risk any light or smoke, but she was cold and hungry. *What do I do now? It would be safest to go back to camp, but what if I led the shooter there? Or got shot on the way?* She was hunting through her backpack when she suddenly stilled, heart racing. Someone was hiking up the hill, breathing hard. They weren't trying to be quiet. *Friend or foe?* Sam relaxed when they continued past her shelter and veered to the west. *How could they have gotten this far up the mountain so early in the morning? Did they camp out as well?* She listened intently until convinced that the noisy hiker was well out of range, then pulled out another protein bar and her bottle of water.

After she ate, Sam put her snowshoes on and followed the tracks until they stopped on the trail ahead. *It's best to know who's around and what they're up to.* Stepping off the path and carefully scanning her environs, she made out a hunting blind in a nearby tree. It was well-camouflaged and bore a marked resemblance to a child's treehouse, with a long ladder running close to the tree's trunk.

Now what? He'll see my tracks if he leaves the same way, and he'll find my refuge. Sam stayed there for a few minutes, undecided about the best course of action, but then elected to hike back the same way and follow the hiker's footprints past her shelter and down the mountainside to the creek. Once she reached the creek, she followed the creek bed to the outcrop where she had exited the day before and looped back to the covert.

Sitting in the shelter's entryway, rummaging through her rucksack for dry socks, Sam stilled. Another person was hiking up the mountain, someone much quieter than the first. She crawled to the edge of the brake and sat on her knees, virtually invisible in her white snowsuit. Her racing heart slowed to a happy thump as she recognized Roger. He plopped his rucksack down and sat on it, looking around.

Sam let out a silent breath of relief. She grinned and immediately wanted to call out to him, but she didn't want to put him in danger or give away her location. Scanning the woods for signs that he had been followed, she finally tossed a small stone in his direction to get his attention. Once he spied her camouflaged location, she motioned him to enter the thicket from the other side, so he slowly made his way, doing his best to brush away his footprints.

Crawling through the brush, he met her inside and gave her a fierce hug. "Nice work on the shelter," he whispered.

"Thanks." She swiped at some moisture around her eyes. "How's Tom? Is he okay?"

Roger nodded. "He was lucky."

"What does that mean?" Sam's eyes widened slightly.

"It means his pack protected him, and his wound isn't fatal."

"Isn't fatal could mean a lot of things."

Roger shrugged. "It hurts. A lot. But it didn't do any permanent damage."

"Is Jack there yet?"

"No. Melissa's looking after Tom right now." He eyed her protein bar and her water. "Why don't you use your Sun Kettle?"

"Good idea. Want some soup? We'll have to eat it quickly, so we don't attract the shooter or any critters with the smell."

"True, but you don't want to starve."

"There are two of us, and we can see them coming. I could really use something warm in my tummy. I'll put water in the other one." She filled the Sun Kettles, opened their solar wings, and set them in the sun to heat.

They were both whispering, but Sam raised a hand when she heard a branch snap. They sat silently for a few moments, waiting, but no sound followed. Sam let out a small breath. "This is nerve-wracking."

"Do you have a plan? Do you want to come back to camp with me?"

She looked at him, her employee, her friend. His short, brown hair was mussed from his hood, and he had bags under his eyes. Her heart swelled, and she shook her head, blinking back the tears that threatened. "I don't want to put anyone else in danger. Art is up here somewhere, trying to help. I think he knows something, but I couldn't get him to tell me when I saw him yesterday. You didn't see anyone on your way here?"

"No, but I left very early."

Sam opened the Sun Kettle and took a sip of soup before handing it to Roger. "Someone hiked by here before you, but they went off to the west. I wondered how they got this far up so early in the morning, and I followed them.

"I saw your tracks, but they were going in the wrong direction. Some people come up here and hunt illegally. They might have a hunting blind or camp nearby." He handed the thermos back to Sam.

"They do. I found the blind, but I have no idea if that person is the shooter or some random person who just happens to be out here. Will you stay here tonight, and we can leave early tomorrow?"

"That's probably a good idea, huh. The two sets of footprints might help confuse anyone who's looking for you. You could head up to the waterfall tomorrow, no?"

Tilting her head, she smiled at his slang and took another drink of soup. "That's a great idea. I have supplies in the cave, and no one will ever find it unless they know it's there."

A hawk flew through the trees and landed on a branch above their heads.

"That's a Cooper hawk," Roger said.

Sam looked up and studied it. From above, it would have blue-gray feathers, but looking up, she could see warm reddish bars on its belly and thick, dark bands on its tail.

"They like to sneak up on their prey and surprise them, kind of like cats. When they go for it, they shoot around tree branches like they're in a death-defying obstacle course."

"No fear."

"Well, that's not entirely true. They're afraid of owls, eagles, and crows." Roger smiled.

"Jack could send them packing." Sam laughed quietly, referring to her cousin's nickname.

"What happened to your arm?"

Sam looked down at the duct tape holding her bloodied jacket sleeve together. "It's just a scratch."

"It bled through your jacket, so it must have been more than a scratch."

"It was an arrow, but it didn't penetrate my arm." She shrugged. "I took care of it."

"Do you want me to look at it?"

"No, it's fine. It's too cold to mess with it right now."

The campers were fidgety after breakfast and full of questions, so Ben decided to take them out for a lesson in foraging. "Please stick together and pay attention. Some plants can be poisonous, so it's important to know which ones you can pick and which ones you can't."

David put his hands on his hips. "I don't know why you all feel the need to treat us like children.

Obviously, we know the dangers of picking the wrong plants." His small stature and belligerent attitude reminded Ben of Napoleon.

"If I assumed everyone knew which plants were poisonous, and someone died because they ate the wrong mushroom or berry, I would be liable, and I would feel terrible. So please let me issue warnings just in case."

David rolled his eyes. "Whatever, man. I'm pretty sure we're all adults here."

Ben felt the familiar pressure in his chest and tried to tell himself to let it go. *I probably should have listened to the doctor, but I really wanted to be here.* He passed around copies of a popular guidebook and some paper bags. "Why don't we start with mushrooms. Never put mushrooms in plastic bags. They make the mushrooms sweat. Also, stay below the clearing because it's illegal to forage for mushrooms on state land."

"Yeah, I read that somewhere," Scott said, nodding.

Ben looked around. "Where are Lisa and Sissy?"

The four remaining campers looked around and shrugged.

"We need to find them before we continue. Let's fan out but stay within voice range."

They separated and went almost to the clearing when they found the two women arguing. Lisa shoved Sissy and started to stomp toward the clearing, her sharp blonde bob gleaming in the sun.

"Eee, she's a mean one," Sissy declared from where she landed.

"Lisa!" Ben's voice boomed. "Please return to the group. We postponed starting to look for you."

"You are not my babysitter. I can go where I like."

"It's not safe at this time, and Roger asked us to stay together. If you are going to leave camp and not follow guidelines, I'll need you to sign a waiver first. Shall we all return to the tents?"

"Man, why do you always have to be causing trouble?" David crossed his arms over his stocky frame.

"I'll sign it later. I need some time alone. Keep *her* away from me."

She pointed at Sissy, who was still sitting in the snow, then left them staring.

"She acts like a total wimp, but she's *strong*."

Everyone looked at Sissy.

"What happened?" Ben asked.

"I saw her walk off, and I followed her. I told her she should stick with the group, but she argued with me and pushed me down."

"Thank you for trying to look out for her. Let's all get back to our lesson and just hope she's careful."

They trudged back to their original location, and Ben began again. "I've bookmarked some mushrooms that can grow during the winter months: Chaga, Turkey Tail, Witches Butter, Artist's Conk, and Lion's Mane are a few. Look around, see if you can spot any. If you do, you can compare them to the pictures in the book, but please don't eat them. We'll go through your finds when we get back to camp and discuss them."

The campers spread out, looking for some of the mushrooms mentioned in their field guides.

Jorge, a local ranch owner, became extremely excited when he discovered a clump of Chaga. "Ben! This is Chaga, no?"

"Yes, it is." He looked up at the black clump growing on a birch tree. The inside was a deep golden color. "Do you know how to harvest it?"

"The book says to use an axe and not to take more than a third so it can continue growing."

"That's right. It grows very slowly, so if you take too much, it will kill the fungus and the tree. Here's my axe. See if you can remove some of it."

Everyone gathered around, and Jorge did an impressive job of harvesting the mushroom.

"I saw a YouTube video about that," Scott nodded.

"Let's talk about some other things we can forage during the winter. We do have some competition, and the forest animals need the food more than we do this week, so leave most of what you find for them."

"We don't have a lot of snowy forests in Burque, but maybe I could take some samples back to show the students." Sissy, a schoolteacher, was always interested in lessons that would keep her students engaged. She bounced on her toes whenever she found something of interest.

Ben nodded.

The group walked through the forest together, Ben pointing out dock seeds, a few stray acorns, papery, y-shaped wings containing maple seeds, and goosefoot seeds clinging to tall, rigid stalks. "You will notice in your field guides that most of these require some work before you eat them. The dock seeds need to be toasted and ground into flour. Maple seeds need to be removed from their wings. Goosefoot seeds, or wild quinoa, must be chaffed. But they are all nutritious and can be used to sustain you."

"Aren't there things we can just pick and eat?" David asked.

"There are, but remember, we're competing with squirrels, who started gathering them much earlier in the year. Black walnuts, beechnuts, pine nuts, and acorns are all good, although you still must remove the husk and shell from the walnuts. Crab apples are also a tasty treat if you can find them. Let's see what else we can find."

David grew bored and started trying to engage Sissy in conversation, but she tossed her long, black hair and turned her back to him, returning to the task at hand. He wandered off, digging up snow with his boots and rustling trees and bushes.

Noticing the campers' attention was waning, Ben called them all back. "Let's return to camp. We can examine the things you found, and I'll get dinner started."

"That sounds good," Scott said.

"You always have something to say, and it never means anything," David scoffed.

Scott shrugged and pulled a joint out of his pocket.

Hailey linked her arm through Scott's and glared at David.

Although very petite, Ben thought her long red hair and ample piercings gave her a fierce look. He ran his fingertips through his small blonde mustache and felt the pressure return to his chest.

Five of the six campers returned to the tents with Ben that afternoon. Tom was dozing, Melissa by his cot on her campstool. "Roger's not back?"

"No," she said softly. "He'll be back tomorrow."

"How do you know?"

She smiled. "I just do."

"Okay, everyone, take your finds to the table and identify them for Melissa. I'll have dinner whipped up in no time," Ben boomed.

Tom opened his eyes groggily. "What time is it?"

"Camping dinner time," Ben said.

"Melissa stole my watch."

"You can't be watching the clock when you're in the sick bay."

"Where's Roger?"

"He's with Sam. He'll be back tomorrow."

Tom frowned a little, creating small lines across his forehead.

"Don't worry. It's not like that. He's helping her ground herself."

"What does that mean?"

"Roger is connected to the land. His presence is helping Sam feel more relaxed and confident, so she can do what needs to be done."

"Where do you come up with these things? Do you just make them up as you go?"

"Maybe." She smiled sweetly.

Tom smiled, too, and shook his head. "Whether you are making them up or not, they are comforting. I hope you're right."

"I am. You'll see." She felt his forehead. "Do you think you're well enough to sit at the table for dinner?"

"I can give it a try."

"Come and get it," Ben boomed.

Everyone got in line and then took their food to the table, except for Tom. He sat at the end nearest his cot, and Melissa brought him his dinner. The campers were a little quiet, but complete silence fell when Lisa entered the tent.

"Glad you made it back! Are you hungry?" Ben handed her a plate.

She took it from him and said, "Thank you. I'm sorry about this afternoon."

Sissy glared at her, but no one made any comments.

"Glad to see you up, man," David addressed Tom. "You weren't hurt too badly?"

Tom grimaced. "Yeah, not too bad."

Melissa noticed he was bleeding again. "We should get you back to bed and redress your wound," she whispered.

He gave a brief nod and clenched his teeth.

Chapter 3

Sam and Roger spent the rest of the day scouting around the shelter and resting.

"Yesterday really wore me out. All the bursts of adrenaline, the long climb with that heavy rucksack, and my injury; plus, I didn't sleep very well."

"It was uncomfortable or what?"

"No, I was just anxious."

"Look, over there." They had followed another set of tracks, and when they rounded the final corner, Roger pointed out a well-camouflaged blind. They backed into the brush so they wouldn't be visible to anyone inside.

"That's the blind I found earlier, but I was traveling in the opposite direction. I wonder where he is."

"And I wonder who he is. Is he the shooter or just a random person who happens to be out here with us?"

"We wouldn't know unless he's carrying a bow, or he tries to shoot us."

He nodded. "Let's loop back to the shelter and not chance meeting up with whoever it is."

They separated and zigzagged back to the shelter, brushing some of their tracks with tree branches, trying not to be obvious about where they were headed. They entered the thicket from opposite sides, on all fours.

"Did you see anyone on your way back?" Roger asked.

"No, I wonder where he is."

Roger shrugged. "Maybe they thought you'd gone farther up the mountain and headed north. If so, you'd better be extra careful tomorrow."

"I will. How about we heat a couple of survival meals in the Sun Kettles, and I found a tiny propane heater in my rucksack when I was going through it this morning. We can have a nice, warm meal and heat up the shelter a little before we sleep."

"Can we both fit in there?" He eyed it skeptically.

"I think so. We'll just have to sleep on our sides." Sam passed him his thermos and a spoon. "Do you remember when we took that trip to the river last Spring?"

"Yeah. That was a good day, huh." He took a bite of instant mac and cheese and scrunched up his face.

"I know it's not the best food in the world, but it's warm and will fill our tummies."

"True."

"Anyway, that day at the river was when I started thinking of you as a friend."

"Yeah, me too. It was the first time I realized you were a real person." He blushed a little, and Sam laughed. "What I mean is…"

"I know what you mean, I think." Sam smiled.

"You always seemed like the princess in the golden palace. I realized that day that you're a regular person, just like me. We both have our happy days and our challenges."

Sam nodded. "I'm glad we're friends now, and I'm glad you're here with me. I was feeling very tired and alone."

"I was worried about you. I'm glad I found you."

Finishing their modest meal, they sealed the Sun Kettles, returned them to their packs and hung the packs in the tree branches. They kept their guns and reflective bags out, and Sam retrieved her mini heater. "If we put the heater in the shelter and sit in front of the entrance, we can block the little bit of light it puts off."

"It's not going to stay warm for long."

"True. And it's not big enough to last all night."

"Taking the chill off is good. We can do the same in the morning, no?"

"Morning is rough." Sam pulled her boots and jacket off and scootched down into her reflective bag, rolling onto her side to make room for Roger. He got into his bag, too, and rolled to face the entrance of the shelter, so he could see anyone or anything that approached. Sam turned off the little heater. "Good night, Roger."

"Good night, Ms. Sam."

"What did I tell you about that?"

"Sorry." He chuckled. "Good night, Sam."

She couldn't see him in the dark, but she could hear the smile in his voice. His presence put her at ease, and she slept soundly that night.

The next morning, they rose again with the dawn. Sam turned the little heater on for a few minutes, and Roger set the unused Sun Kettle out to boil some water. "I have a feeling you'd like some coffee, no?" he whispered.

"I would like coffee more than anything else. You are a god send." She sat up in her reflective bag and put on her jacket. After it had warmed her up, she added the boots and took a deep breath. "Today's going to be a hike."

"I hate to leave you up here alone."

"I'll be fine now, and you'll know where to find me."

"True. Be careful with the coffee. You can smell it for miles."

"Let's just keep the cap on except when we're taking a drink."

They shared the coffee and got their packs reorganized. Roger gave Sam his extra food and water, and an extra pair of dry socks.

"Thank you, Roger." She hugged him hard, her watery eyes belying her smile.

"I'll always be there for you. Take care of yourself, and I'll see you on the other side of this."

They scanned the area around the shelter before she headed north, and he tromped in multiple directions before heading back down the mountain. Continuing downhill, using his poles and the sides of his snowshoes to stay upright, Roger stopped suddenly behind a tree when he heard murmuring. He strained his ears, trying to figure out where the voice was coming from, and thought two people might be having a whispered argument, but he could only catch a word here and there. He caught the word *found* and another *why*; the majority of the conversation floated off into the breeze. He decided it would be better to continue back to camp rather than try to confront whoever it was. Maybe he could find out who was missing from camp, and if it was the shooter, at least they were down here and not following Sam. *Is that wrong? Maybe I should try to climb up into a tree. But what if they hear me? Trying to fend off two, armed people from up in a tree would be a losing proposition.*

Hiking steadily uphill and to the east, Sam didn't need to rest as much since she wasn't running, and she moved more quietly. Paying close attention to any unusual sounds or smells and looking for tracks, she felt the solitude and then the vibrant life surrounding her. *Life in the forest has its own rhythm, its own sounds, and smells.*

Her body was tired, but she could distinguish the rock formation that housed the waterfall in the distance. Sitting on a boulder near the edge of the forest, she breathed in deeply, trying to identify the natural smells around her. Partially camouflaged by the snow, she could smell the earth, pine trees, moldy leaves, and damp animal fur. *I wonder how far away that animal is and what it is. I should get Roger to teach me about tracking.*

If she concentrated, Sam could hear the forest as well. She heard the Cooper Hawk before she saw it and the squeal of a rabbit as it dashed into the dense shrubs. She heard the light breeze whistling through the tops of the pines and the burbling sound of the river ahead.

Rather than approach the waterfall directly, she headed to the east, across a glade, and joined the small river that fed the falls. She entered the half-frozen river and waded along the edge to the top of the waterfall, where she lay and rested in the snow. Rolling over onto her sore arm, she sucked in a breath at the shooting pain but continued rolling until she was on her belly, propped up on her elbows. From her vantage point, she could see the forest in every direction. She stayed there for a long time, scanning the landscape for threats.

When she was sure no one had followed her, Sam army crawled in reverse to the steep path that led to the base waterfall, brushing away her tracks as she went. Descending was a scramble, and at the bottom, she located the narrow, overgrown path behind a wall of tall bushes that led to a cave entrance behind the falls.

She shifted a jury-rigged wooden fence she had placed over the narrow mouth of the cave. Although she knew that animals or people could get through if they wanted to, she had never found the cave occupied, nor the fence moved, on any of her previous visits.

Moving quietly through the cave, she checked for smaller visitors, like snakes. The larger, central cavity sported a fire ring she had constructed many years ago. Two smaller cavities behind the first were also empty, save for a woven mat she had made, a locked food safe in one corner, and a few supplies she was testing. The second cove held dry wood for the fire.

Sam smiled. The food safe contained additional supplies, including a bottle of whiskey. She couldn't afford to become inebriated, but a shot of whiskey might just chase the chills away.

Having sent the two dirty Sun Kettles back with Roger in exchange for his two clean ones, Sam went about filling them with water and setting them to heat in the sun outside the cave. She still couldn't have a fire, but in the innermost cave, she would be able to use her small heater and a weak lantern. The cave was warmer, too, because it was underground and protected from the wind. Sam smiled. *Great idea, Roger.*

Chapter 4

Upon returning to camp, Roger discovered everyone except Tom and Melissa were gone. Red bounded toward the door wagging his tail vigorously when Roger walked in. "You missed me, huh. I missed you too." He gave his canine friend a treat and a scratch, then focused his attention on Tom, who was still in pain and worried about Sam. "Don't worry, old man. I found her and made sure she has extra supplies. She'll be fine."

Tom pressed his lips together and scrunched his eyebrows.

"Where are the others?" Roger looked at Melissa.

"Ben took them out for a campfire cooking lesson. They were all getting irritable."

Roger frowned. "We need to form a buddy system." He straightened suddenly and cocked his head. "I hear an engine. Be right back." Loping out of the tent with Red on his heels, Roger nearly collided with Jack. "Thank goodness you're here! Where's the snowmobile?"

"Anita dropped me off and had to get back."

Roger's shoulders slumped. "How are you at backwoods first aid?"

"What kind of first aid?"

"Tom's been shot with an arrow."

"Who's Tom?"

Roger stared at him. *She hasn't told him?* "Uh... the detective Sam met in Las Vegas?"

Jack squinted. "She has always been good at making friends. Lead the way."

They entered the first tent and Jack was surprised by how warm and roomy it was. Sam told him about the two hot tents she had bought, but he hadn't seen them. A wood stove, a long table, chairs, and several cots were arranged inside. Melissa was sitting on a camp chair next to one of the cots, the one Tom was lying on. He was on his side and wore a grimace of pain.

"Tom, this is Jack. He's a doctor."

Tom gave a weak smile. "Sam's cousin. I've heard a lot about you."

Jack nodded but frowned a little, removing his snow suit. "Let's take a look at that wound, and you can tell me what happened."

He sat on the edge of the bed and ran his hand through his thick, black hair. He had imagined a different type of arrival. He pulled on a pair of surgical gloves and carefully rolled Tom a little bit forward so he could see his back. Removing the bandaging, Jack could see that the arrow had just missed Tom's spine. "You were lucky, but you could probably use some stitches." He touched the side of the wound and put his fingers to his nose. "Is that honey?"

"Yes. It's a natural antibiotic."

Jack looked at Melissa, the local plant and herb specialist and Sam's best friend. "You're pretty sharp. Did you give him something for pain?"

"Bromelain."

Jack nodded. He took Tom's temperature and blood pressure. "So, what happened?"

"Sam and I were scouting for the next day's lesson. She went ahead and gave me directions to see if the average camper could find the location. I was crossing a clearing and saw her enter the tree line above, then she disappeared. I stopped to figure out where she went when something hit me in the back, and I fell forward. I think I might have been unconscious for a while. I'm not sure, but my back felt like it was on fire, and I couldn't get up."

"Sam let off a flare and covered us while we helped Tom get out of the clearing," Roger added.

"Where is she now?"

"She's safe. I went to find her and stayed overnight. We scouted around a little, and she went on up to a place she knows."

Jack had to leave the tent. He walked outside and let the cold shock him out of the instant, intense panic he suffered. Sam was out there alone, and there was nothing he could do about it. Or maybe there was. He needed more information.

He walked back inside and said, "Roger, we need to talk."

Roger walked back outside with Jack. "What is it? Is Tom in danger?"

Jack shook his head. "I don't think so. You guys did a good job of moving him and patching him up. I am more worried about Sam at the moment. Why didn't you bring her back?"

"She's hiding out. I think we have to trust her and try to figure out the who and the why."

"Are you crazy?" Jack whispered angrily. "She could get injured."

"We also have to keep an eye on Tom and the campers. There were three of us, four with you here. I don't know who we can trust."

"You think one of the campers is the shooter?"

"It's possible."

"Who knew about the camp location?"

"I have no idea. The camp was widely publicized, but not the exact location. I haven't heard any vehicles. Also, there were some incidents when we first arrived."

"Incidents?"

"Things that were done to purposely sabotage the camp."

"For example?"

"One night, someone left the food locker open. No one had any business getting into it, and everyone was told to keep food put away because of bears."

Jack nodded. "Potentially dangerous."

Roger paced. "The next incident was even more obvious. Someone threw several loaded weapons onto the campfire."

"Was anyone hurt?"

"No, but if someone had bent to retrieve them, it could have been deadly."

"The third incident was just bizarre. Someone took Melissa's bag and hid it behind the outhouse tent. I have no idea why."

"Maybe they thought she had drugs."

Roger shrugged. "Anyway, yesterday, someone was shooting arrows at Sam. Maybe they thought shooting Tom would draw her out."

"The sabotage didn't work, so they're trying it a different way?"

"That's what I'm thinking."

Jack ran a hand through his hair. "Introduce me to the campers this evening, and we'll hear from Ben about their day. Then we can have a little staff meeting after dinner. Have you arranged a buddy system?"

"Not really. Sam was going to do that when she got back."

"Okay, let's go back inside. I'm going to stitch Tom up so his wound will heal more quickly." He returned to the tent. "Melissa, can you help me sterilize Tom's wound?"

He scrutinized Tom. "How is your pain tolerance?"

"I'd say it's pretty high, based on his reaction when Roger removed the arrow tip."

Tom smiled weakly at Melissa. "What I'm wondering is if pain is cumulative. It already hurts. Am I to understand you'll be using a needle and thread to sew it up?"

Jack nodded somberly.

"When Roger removed the arrow, Melissa poured some alcohol on it first… and gave me a shot." Tom laughed. "Maybe we could try that again."

"At best, the burn will be so intense it might distract you."

"Two shots then. Let's get it done."

Melissa poured him his shots and sterilized the area on his back while Jack pulled on his surgical gloves and prepared his instruments. She handed Tom a bowl.

"What's this for?"

"Just in case," she said.

Jack handed her some gauze and bandaging and motioned for her to pour some of the alcohol on Tom's wound, which caused Tom to suck in his breath.

"I'll try to be as quick as I can."

Tom clenched his teeth.

Jack finished with the stitches, and Tom threw up in the bowl. "Great job, Tom. You're tough; I'll give you that." Jack put his instruments in a baggie to be sterilized later and stood, removing his gloves.

Melissa wiped Tom's mouth and took the bowl from him. "You did great." She patted his arm.

Roger stuck his head in the tent. "Looks like they're returning."

Jack joined him outside.

"Hello, Jack!" Ben boomed.

Jack held up a hand and smiled.

"Welcome back. Did you make something delicious?" Roger asked.

"I think we have. What do you think, folks?"

Everyone agreed, some more enthusiastically than others.

"Who's he?" David asked, pointing at Jack.

"Jack's a late arrival. We'll go inside and introduce ourselves while Ben figures out how to divvy up your delicacies."

As Ben cooked up one of his five-star dinners, incorporating the food the campers cooked outdoors, Roger gathered everyone around the table. "Since we have a little time, I'd like to introduce all of you to Jack. He's a doctor, and we're glad he could make it. Could each of you introduce yourself: name, where you're from, what you do for a living and why you came to this camp? Then, I'll let Jack tell you about himself. Let's start with you, Scott, and go around the table clockwise."

He stood, wobbled, and bumped the table, his brown eyes dilated. "Hi. I'm Scott Jacobs, and this is my wife, Hailey. We just moved to Santo Milagro and love the outdoors."

"We're starting a small farm and hope to sell produce and homemade breads and jams," Hailey added, her piercings catching and reflecting the light from the lantern overhead.

"Why did you sign up for survival training?" Jack asked.

"We wanted to learn more about this place and how to survive if we get lost or hurt," Scott said.

Hailey nodded. "I'm interested in plants and natural remedies."

"You can learn a lot from Melissa. She's our resident expert." Roger smiled at Melissa, who blushed slightly.

"I hope you'll have time to teach me a few things," Hailey smiled shyly at Melissa.

Jorge stood next. "Hola. I'm Jorge Sanchez. I own a ranch on the east side of Santo Milagro. I've known Sam most of my life and thought it would be cool to check out her new venture."

"Are you related to Señor Sanchez, who owns the hardware store?" Jack asked.

"I am." Jorge smiled with even, white teeth. "He's my great uncle." He tamped down his black mustache and looked to his left.

Sissy stood and focused her dark eyes on Jack. Although petite, she exuded considerable energy and spoke in a high-pitched voice. "My name is Sissy Wong. I'm a school teacher in Burque. I heard about this training from a friend of mine. The children love to be outdoors, and I thought I could learn practical skills to use in our lessons."

Jack looked at her and blinked. *I can't believe it. How did she know I'd be here?*

"And what do you think so far?" Roger asked.

"I'm learning so many things! Various kinds of knots, outdoor cooking, making a fire. I can't wait to learn about making a shelter. They will love that!"

"Lucky kids to have such an enthusiastic teacher."

Roger looked at the next camper, tall and fit with a severe blonde bob. "How about you, Lisa?" He prompted.

"Hi," she said shyly. "My name is Lisa Carson. I work in an office in Las Rodillas. I'm not sure why I came." She shrugged. "I guess I thought my life was pretty boring and that this would be fun."

"And is it?" Jack asked, spotting her feet, which appeared almost as big as his.

"I guess so. It's kind of hard sometimes." Her sharp eyes and her words are at odds.

A short, stocky man with straight brown hair jumped up and said, "My name is David Arndt. I'm an amateur survivalist. I post a lot on Instagram and YouTube, and I thought this might be good for my channels."

Roger asked. "So, you didn't really expect to learn anything?"

David shrugged. "If I do, that's great. If I don't, no harm. I did learn some stuff from Ben today. Now, how about you, doc?"

Jack raised a single eyebrow as he gazed at the brash young man. "Well, Roger told you I'm a doctor. I'm a medical examiner from Albuquerque. Sam asked me to come in case anyone needed medical aid. And it seems someone did. What do you all think about this?" He gestured toward Tom.

"I think it was very painful," Tom grumbled.

"You're all patched up now, and I'll monitor the wound for signs of infection."

Everyone nodded, and Tom scowled.

"That's not what I meant, though. I meant, what do you think happened, and where do you think Sam is?"

"I think she was probably the one who shot him," Lisa said.

Tom jerked back in surprise. "Why would she do that? She loves me."

Jack bit his tongue and stared at Tom.

"Maybe she saw you flirting with Sissy." She crossed her arms.

"I didn't." Tom rolled his eyes.

"Not helping," Jack said.

"Maybe she crossed sacred Native American soil, and one of them shot her," Scott said.

"This is government land," Roger said. "Besides, it was Tom who got shot."

"Could be a hunter with bad aim," Jorge suggested.

"Then where is Sam?" Lisa asked. "I bet she did it. I read a book where the main character—"

"Seriously, Lisa, you are so annoying," David pounded the table with his fist.

"Dinner's ready," Ben boomed. "Who's hungry?"

Jack sat for a moment, lost in thought as the others stood and formed a line.

He looked at Tom, who seemed to be studying him. He had to find Sam for more than one reason. *She belongs with me, and I need her to be safe and well. I'm such an idiot.* He stood and joined the back of the line.

"Ben, you've outdone yourself," Melissa said after her first bite. "This is delicious."

Jack agreed. The steak was tender and juicy, cooked with sauteed mushrooms and garlic. The wild lettuce salad was tart, with a sweet and sour dressing, and the mashed potatoes were creamy, with just enough lumps to give them texture.

When dinner was almost over, Jack said, "Roger tells me that Sam was planning to establish a buddy system when she got back. I think that we should go ahead and do that now. Anyone who leaves camp or separates from the group should have their buddy with them. Do any of you have a strong preference, or should we draw names?"

"Can Hailey and I be buddies?" Scott asked.

Jack nodded.

"Then, I'd like to be buddies with Jorge," David said.

"Shouldn't we team up with the women for their safety?" Jorge asked.

Jack pondered that question. "Ideally, everyone should stick together."

"I don't mind being partners with Lisa."

"Thanks, Sissy." Jack thought Lisa sounded sarcastic, but Sissy smiled amiably.

"So, everyone is okay with those arrangements?"

Everyone nodded.

"Melissa, you and Tom can be buddies. Ben, Roger, and I can alternate as needed. Now, a couple of ground rules."

"Why are you making up rules?" David asked belligerently.

"For our safety. If you go anywhere, even the restroom, and don't take your buddy, let someone know where you're going."

They looked at each other.

"That sounds reasonable," Jorge said. "What's the other one?"

"Tomorrow, you will learn how to shoot. If you and your buddy go off on your own, take a rifle with you and keep your eyes open."

"I don't want to shoot anyone!" Lisa said.

"Hopefully, you won't have to. Perhaps just seeing you have a weapon will prevent an attack."

Sissy patted Lisa's arm. "It's okay. I know how to shoot."

Lisa recoiled and jerked her arm away.

Jack stood and walked over to Ben, who was cleaning up the pots and pans. "Need any help?"

"No, thanks. I'm about done here, then the campers each wash their own dishes."

"Sounds like a good system."

"The men, except for Tom and Scott, sleep in the second tent. I'll be in to start the fire in a minute unless you and Roger want to get it started."

"Sure. We can do that." He turned. "Roger, we have a mission."

Roger lit a gas lamp, and the two walked the short distance to the second tent. Once they entered the tent, Jack asked, "Do you have a plan? Do you know where Sam is headed?"

"Working on it. We should probably send someone for help, but it's a long hike down the mountain and would be safer with two people. With Tom injured and Sam away, we don't have enough reliable bodies."

Ben entered the tent and started laying kindling in the stove.

"I guess we were too slow," Jack said.

"Did anyone leave the group while you were out?" Roger asked.

Ben didn't look at him. "They were all over the place. I'm only one person. All of them were gone at one point or another. I found the Jacobs smoking a joint behind a tree."

Roger sighed. "Maybe the buddy system will help."

David and Jorge entered the tent and moved to their cots. "There's an extra cot and blankets over in the corner," Roger told Jack. "I'm just going to pop next door and see if anyone needs anything."

Jack looked at Ben with a raised eyebrow.

"I think he might have a thing for Melissa," Ben said.

Jack looked at him carefully. "Are you feeling okay, Ben?"

"Sure. Why?"

"Can I take your blood pressure?"

"I'd rather you didn't."

"Have you been to see a doctor recently?"

"Yes."

There was a pause.

"Is there something you're not telling me?"

"Maybe. Can I just keep it private?"

"If you want. As long as you're aware of it. Don't gamble with your health, Ben."

"Okay, boss."

Jack smiled slightly and went to set up his cot.

Once everyone got settled, the night was still. Jack lay in his cot and listened to symphonic snoring and the occasional coyote's howl. The moon was bright and made the top of the tent glow. He fell asleep thinking of Sam.

He could see her bright smile and feel her warm hug. Then, he thought about how she had cried when he left Santo Milagro that first time. He thought about her silence when he told her he couldn't give up his job. *If I find her safe and she'll have me, I'll give it up. She's more important than some stupid job. Please be okay, Sam.*

Sitting on her woven mat in the cave, Sam felt uncomfortable and alone. She was safer and warmer than she had been in the shelter on the side of the mountain, but she somehow felt more vulnerable, isolated. The cave felt like an alternate reality. Oddly, she wanted to know what was happening outside of her cave-universe. Art's behavior was puzzling. *Why wouldn't he tell me who the shooter was? Why did he think he could get between the shooter and me? He didn't want me to meet his partner. Is his partner the shooter? That seems a little farfetched, but it could possibly explain the sabotage. Why would someone do things that could harm others? And why take Melissa's bag? Were they looking for drugs? What about the campers? Is there anyone I don't trust? They all gave irrefutable backgrounds, but everyone has secrets.*

She prepared for bed, then got into her reflective bag because getting on her knees on the hard ground would likely do some damage. She turned off the tiny heater and the light and closed her eyes. *Father, I don't know why I forget to talk to you when my problems escalate. I'm sorry that I leave you out when the going gets tough. Thank you for keeping me safe and thank you for looking after Tom. Please help me understand what's happening. Help me to trust in you and guide me in finding a solution. Amen.* She crossed herself and fell asleep, feeling the burden lifted from her shoulders.

Chapter 5

The next morning, after a hearty breakfast, Roger and Jack gathered the campers and tromped through the snow to the makeshift shooting range east of their camp. Roger began their lesson by explaining general gun safety. "Can anyone tell us the most important range rule?"

Jorge tentatively held up a hand. "Always point your weapon down range or at the ground—never up or at a person."

"Right." Roger nodded. "If you forget everything else, remember that rule." He continued with the lesson, pointing out the safety on one of the rifles. "You have to release the safety before you can pull the trigger, and you have to cock the gun before you can put it back on safety." He demonstrated before handing each camper a rifle. "Each of you try it a couple of times while the rifles are unloaded."

"It's so heavy," Hailey said. "Are all rifles this heavy?"

"I'm afraid so." No one else mentioned the weight. He returned to the front of the group. "You can load the cartridge here." He demonstrated again, then passed out cartridges. "Go ahead and load your rifle, then take the cartridge out and reload." After everyone had become familiar with their weapons, he asked, "Any questions?"

"Yeah, how do we hit the target?" Hailey asked.

David began to laugh, then stopped suddenly when Roger caught his eye.

"Good question. All the rifles are the same, so we don't have to worry about using the wrong ammunition. They all have a peep sight. You will notice a round hole near your eye. Center the target in that sight, then bring the front sight, here" —he indicated the sight on his rifle— "into the center of the hole. Form a line, and I'll come along and help anyone who needs it."

The targets were numbered one through six. Scott was already standing near number one, so he took his position. Hailey took number two. Mark stood at number three, with Jorge next to him. Lisa took number five, then Sissy stood at number six.

Jack stood back and observed as Roger started at number one, closest to Hailey.

"Do you think you have the hang of it?" Roger asked Scott.

"Oh, yeah. No problem." He nodded vigorously but made no move to shoot his weapon.

Roger nodded and moved to help Hailey. He noted Scott was watching as well. "You can get down on one knee if it helps steady your aim," he said. "Place the butt of your rifle here against your shoulder, and make sure you hold it firmly with both hands. Good. Now tilt your head so you can see the target through the hole."

Hailey followed his instructions and missed the target completely when the recoil surprised her. "I didn't know what you meant," she whispered.

"Good job. Keep practicing, and you'll be a pro in no time."

"Thanks, Roger." She smiled.

He stood back and watched as both Scott and Hailey began to practice.

"You can give back up advice, Jack" Roger nodded his head toward number one as he continued to number three.

David and Jorge waved him on, so he stood back and observed for a few minutes until he determined that they were proficient. His eyebrows rose slightly at David's excellent aim. *Not bad for a YouTuber.* While he was watching David and Jorge, his eyes were drawn to Lisa, who braced for the recoil, unloaded her magazine, and automatically reloaded without thought. *She's a pro. Why tell us she's a beginner?* Roger scratched his chin. Sissy also denied needing any help, but he showed her how to keep better control of her rifle when she fired. He strode back down the line, offering Jorge a tip on better accuracy, then heard Lisa's high, strident voice next to him ringing out over the gunfire.

He turned and heard, "Why do you keep interfering in my business?"

Sissy got right in her face. "I just don't understand why you keep lying to everyone."

"Lying about what? Leave me alone." Lisa threw her rifle down and shoved her away.

"You obviously know how to shoot, no? You're better than me. Why are you lying?"

"Mind your own business if you know what's good for you."

Roger stepped between the two ladies. "If we want the buddy system to work, we need to cooperate. The two of you are obviously not compatible. Lisa, why don't you team up with Jorge? David, you can be Sissy's buddy."

"I want to be Jack's partner." She bounced over to him and took his arm.

"Sorry, Jack's part of the staff, so he's not available."

"Jorge, then." She pouted.

"Fine. Sissy and Jorge. David and Lisa. Jorge, why don't you and Lisa exchange targets, and we'll practice for another half an hour."

After practice, Roger handed out cleaning kits and instructions. "We'll be coming out for target practice regularly, and we need to make sure we take care of our weapons. Let's go through it together the first time, so everyone knows how to properly field strip their rifle. The first and most crucial step is to remove your magazine. Remember the range rules? Point your rifle in a safe direction when you remove the ammunition." He walked them through using their utility brushes and cleaning swabs, demonstrating the application of the cleaner. "You can use swabs to clean areas that are hard to reach."

As the amount of debris decreased significantly, Roger showed the campers how to apply lubrication sparingly and wipe down the components. He then inspected each rifle before returning them to the campers. "Is everyone ready for lunch?"

"Yes!" came the resounding reply.

While Roger was putting the rifles away, Jack approached him as if on a mission. "What's up?"

Jack motioned him away from the tents, then whispered, "I have a problem and a request."

Roger studied him. "Problem first."

"The camper named Sissy." Jack's eyebrows furrowed. "I know her, sort of. She's a stalker. I don't know how she knew I would be here, but she came to our tent last night and wanted to talk."

"Should I have a word with her?"

"That's where we come to the request. It would take care of two problems. Do you know of a cave Sam liked to go to with Ghost?"

"Behind the waterfall?"

"Yes. I want to go. Do you know how to get there?"

"It's quite a distance, but that's where she was headed. She built a shelter about halfway there where you can rest. Let me see if I can draw you a map." He looked Jack in the eye. "You'll want snowshoes, and you'll want to make sure you don't lead the shooter to her."

Jack's pulse quickened. Roger was right. "How do I make sure I don't?"

"Keep your eyes and ears open. I'll give you an indirect route. She might see you from a distance. I don't want anyone to realize you're gone. Let's go out for a snowshoe lesson. I'll take you to the shelter and explain about the map and the snowshoes on the way. We all take packs when we go out, just in case. Grab some lunch, and I'll assemble our gear."

"Thanks, Roger." Jack went inside to get something to eat. "Feeling any better, Ben?"

"Yes. The rest helped a lot, and I took my medication for a change."

Jack nodded. "Good man."

He ate quickly and went to the second tent to find Roger, who handed him a pistol and hefted him a rucksack.

"Ready?"

"I'm not honestly sure, but I have to try," Jack said.

"Put these on." Roger handed him a pair of snowshoes, mimicking attaching the snowshoes securely to his boots, then handed him two poles. "You can fold them and put them in your pack if you need to, but they can help a lot, especially if you fall."

Jack slipped the gun into his pocket and took the poles.

They walked out into the snow, and Jack mirrored how Roger walked with his feet separated enough so the snowshoes didn't overlap. By the time they had crossed the clearing, he felt like he was getting the hang of it.

"When we go uphill, dig your toes in so the crampons can grip the snow."

Jack tried that, flapped his arms as he began to fall forward, overcompensated, and ended up on his back.

"This is good, no? You can practice getting up."

"This is insane. I'm never going to make it."

"You can do it, but it's lucky we know where Sam's shelter is. You don't want to overdo it the first day. I'll help you get set up before I head back."

"I wish you could go all the way to the cave with me," Jack said with a grimace. "How do I get up?"

"Roll over onto your front."

Jack did as he was instructed.

"Now push yourself back onto your knees. Yep. Now put one foot flat on the ground with your knee up and use your legs and the poles to help you get to your feet."

"Now I understand why you said the poles are helpful." Jack grinned. "The pack adds a lot of extra weight."

Roger continued moving. "If the mountain becomes too steep, you can sidestep. Stand sideways, edge your snowshoe into the snow, and stamp." He showed Jack how to plant the edge of his snowshoe into the snow, heel first, then toe, pause, then transfer his weight to the toe.

"Next, bring your second foot up next to the first and take another step. Just make sure you have space between your steps, so they don't cave in." He took five steps up, then waited for Jack to follow.

Jack was breathing hard by the time he caught up.

"Don't worry. You'll get the hang of it, and it will get easier."

Jack shook his head. "I don't know, Roger."

"You can make switchbacks like when you're hiking if it gets very steep. And don't back up. If you need to go back, turn around in a small circle."

The mountain flattened slightly, and Jack smiled.

"Let's zigzag a bit and stick to the trees."

Jack had to stop and rest more often than he wanted to. "I feel like such a wimp," he said dejectedly.

"It's hard work snowshoeing uphill, even without the heavy pack. You're doing fine."

"It seems awfully quiet up here. Do you think the shooter followed Sam further uphill?"

"Maybe. Sam said Art was up here, too, running interference. That guy." Roger shook his head. "He gives stealth a whole new meaning. You don't see or hear him unless he wants you to."

"Who's Art?"

"You've been away for too long." Roger laughed. "Art is Sam's survival instructor. He's crazy good."

"I've been a rotten friend. I was so embroiled in my work that I wasn't paying attention."

"Well, now you can sit in a cave and catch up. Here's the shelter," Roger whispered. "Loop around to the other side so we don't disturb the snow here." He showed Jack how to crawl into the thicket from the side, then led him to the shelter.

Chapter 6

Jorge helped Tom to the table while Melissa napped. Ben took them each a beer and sat down as well. David shuffled the cards. He looked up at Tom. "How're you doing, man?"

"It's a little better. No tag football or anything, but at least I can sit at the table."

David nodded. "Five-card draw?"

Everyone agreed, so he began dealing the cards.

"What are we playing for?" Jorge asked.

"How about beef jerky." Tom winked. "Everyone could use more jerky."

"Brilliant." Ben smiled. "Blue chips are one piece of jerky; red chips are a package."

Tom won the first hand.

They were on the second hand when Sissy entered the tent and looked around. "Where's Jack?"

Ben looked up. "He and Roger went for a snowshoe lesson since Jack missed that one. Is there something I can help you with?"

She frowned. "No, I just wanted to talk to him." She hung around for a few minutes, then left without saying anything more.

"I thought she was the normal one in our group, but she's just as weird as the rest of us," David said.

"I'm not weird," Jorge said.

"Yes, you are. You hardly ever say anything."

"Nothing wrong with that," Tom said. "Anyone know where Lisa went?"

"She's supposed to be my partner," David said. "She told me to get lost."

Jorge nodded. "Sissy is my partner now. No way I'm leaving this game to babysit her. I need the jerky."

Admiring the sturdy, well-built shelter Jack whispered, "Sam made this?"

"Yeah. We're supposed to be having a class on building emergency shelters tomorrow."

"I'm impressed."

Roger nodded. "She did an excellent job." He shifted his focus to Jack's backpack. "I mostly packed food and water for you and Sam, but if you take off your pack, I'll show you a couple of extra things you can use tonight. It gets very cold out here, especially when you aren't moving around."

"It's already well below freezing."

Roger eyed him with trepidation, then opened the pack and started pulling a few things from the top. "Here's an extra shirt and a pair of dry socks." He handed them to Jack and pulled out a small, shiny roll about the size of a large jar of spaghetti sauce. "This is especially important. Take care of it."

"What is it?"

"It's a reflective bag. It's very thin and packs small, but it will save your life out here. Get inside it at night and pull it up over your head. It will trap your body heat inside and keep you warm."

Jack nodded.

"I recommend removing your boots and jacket before you get in, so you don't feel as cold in the morning. Also, Sam told me about these tiny heaters." He extracted a small heating element and screwed it onto a miniature propane tank before handing it to Jack. "She had one with her, and that extra warmth made the shelter a little more comfortable before bed and first thing.

I added some extra propane containers because they're small and don't last very long. You have an extra Sun Kettle. Sam has two. It can heat food or water using the sun." Roger shrugged. "That's about it, except for a small first aid kit, some rope, a knife. Like I said, it's mostly food and water."

"Thank you, Roger. I really appreciate this."

Roger nodded. "Here's the map I made for you. When you get to the creek, walk on the stones until you see the outcrop of boulders, then cover your tracks as you move toward them. Remember to keep your eyes and ears open."

"What does Art look like? In case I run into him."

"He is about your height and very muscular, bald but probably wearing a hat, so that won't help. It's unlikely you'll see or hear him unless he wants you to."

"Okay." Jack nodded. "You're leaving now?"

"Yes, I'd like to get back before dark. Take care of yourself and be careful about noise, light, and smoke. You've got this."

Jack let out a deep breath. "I'll do my best." Roger clapped him on the back, then crawled out of the thicket, leaving Jack to rummage in his pack for lunch.

Sam spent the day scouting around the waterfall. After scanning the woods from the top, she returned downstream and worked her way around the perimeter of the woods. *They don't seem to have come this far. Strange. I wonder where they are. Have they given up?* She climbed a tree and sat for a while, listening and taking solace from the forest. Rabbits, deer, and foxes busily went about their business, ignoring her presence overhead. She saw the Cooper hawk again, sitting high in a neighboring tree, watching for prey. *I wonder if it's the same one.* She had the fanciful thought that he might be following her. *Then she shivered. That would be creepy.* She thought the shooters might be like the hawk, sitting, watching, waiting. Then she shivered again.

When she returned to the cave, it was getting late, and she was hungry. *I sure would like a nice, juicy steak… or pizza… anything other than survival food.* She had put most of the food and water in the food locker to lighten her rucksack, so she perused the contents to see if anything appealed to her. *I should be grateful I have something warm and filling to eat.* Filling her Sun Kettles with soup and water, she set them out to heat before the sun went down. *I wish I had a book.* She sighed. *Things could be worse. I need to figure out where the shooter went so I can catch him and get back to camp.*

After she finished her modest meal, Sam turned on the small heater and carefully unwrapped her arm. Her wound had reopened and bled a couple of times, but it didn't look infected, so she applied more antibiotic ointment and redressed it. She sniffed and wrinkled her nose as she put her shirt and jacket back on. *Augh. I can smell myself. I wish I could take a bath.* Then she shivered violently, thinking about how cold that would be. *Better warm than clean.*

After helping herself to a warming shot of whiskey, she leaned against the wall of the cave and felt replete. *I wish Tom was here with me. We could talk for hours and snuggle up at night when we're cold.* Her eyes started to droop, so she turned off the little heater and slid into her reflective bag. As soon as she was ready for bed, her body decided she wasn't sleepy anymore. *That figures. What should I do tomorrow?* She pondered the possibilities, then finally said a prayer and drifted off to sleep. She dreamt of a hawk with bright blue eyes, glistening with merriment, then the eyes transformed into the deep gray hue of the sky during inclement weather. The hawk followed her through darkened woods, waiting for something. What was it waiting for?

Taking an alternate route back down the hill, Roger thought he was being vigilant and was shocked to see Art suddenly standing before him on the trail. He flinched. "Where did you come from? I can't ever see you until you appear."

Art gave a low chuckle. "Was that Jack you brought up here?"

Roger nodded.

"Is he heading in Sam's direction?"

"Yeah."

"I'll look out for him. I need to talk to Sam anyway."

"Thanks. He's new to this."

"Got it. He'll be fine. Head down that way." Art pointed to the east and disappeared into the trees.

Roger stood staring in the direction Art went but couldn't see him anywhere. *If I didn't know him, it would spook me when he disappears like that. It kind of spooks me anyway.* He turned and continued down the hill, veering in the direction Art had indicated.

As he approached the eastern side of the clearing, Roger saw David hiding behind a tree, watching Lisa return to camp. He was moving slowly and quietly. Lisa was exiting the west side of the clearing, looking around and walking with purpose.

Roger walked up behind David and put his hand on his shoulder. The small squeal and jump alerted Roger that he had scared him and of course, the hand on his chest. "What's up?"

After several deep breaths, David frowned. "Why did you do that? You almost made me pee myself."

"Just practicing. Why are you spying on Lisa?"

"She keeps telling me to go away and ditching camp. I want to know what she's up to."

"Did you find out?"

"No, not really. I lost her for a while."

"Interesting. Want to walk back together?"

"Might as well. I've lost her now anyway. Where've you been? Ben said you were giving Jack a snowshoe lesson."

"I was, yes."

David looked at him but didn't ask any more questions.

They walked in silence for a while, then Roger said, "Have you noticed anything strange since we've been here? Other than Lisa's disappearing act?"

"All of us are a little different," David said slowly. "Me included."

"How so?"

"You know how I said I'm a YouTuber?"

"Aren't you?"

"I am, but no one watches my channel. Maybe I'm boring or not good looking enough." He shrugged. "Anyway, I live with my grandmother, and she's started telling me I should get a real job, but I'm desperate to make this work."

"What about the others?"

"Well, Scott smokes pot… all the time. I wouldn't ever give him a gun or any kind of weapon, for that matter. Hailey is afraid of something. Not Scott. Something else. And even though he acts like a know it all, he does whatever she tells him to."

"Sissy?"

"She's got a fixation with Jack… and Lisa for some reason."

"Jorge seems pretty normal."

"He's just so quiet and stoic. I can't figure him out."

Roger laughed. "I think he's just a regular guy who's trying something new."

"Maybe. I bet he's got something going on in that head of his."

"You might have missed your calling. You'd make a good investigative reporter."

David raised his eyebrows. "If I have to go out and get a regular job, I'll keep that in mind."

"Do you know much about building shelters?"

"Oh, yeah. That's one of my favorite things to do."

"Good. Maybe you can assist tomorrow and do some filming while you're at it."

David smiled. "Thanks."

They walked into camp and found everyone in line for dinner. "Good timing. What's cooking, Ben?"

"Rabbit stew. I had some time on my hands."

Roger rubbed his stomach. "One of my favorites. Do you think Red might have a few bites as well? He's been eating them raw."

"I think we might have a little left for him.

Chapter 7

Having finished his evening meal, a sandwich Ben had packed for him and some soup he had heated up earlier, Jack stretched and tried to meditate. He went to bed early and lay with his eyes open, listening to the sounds of the forest. In Albuquerque, it was not unusual to hear traffic, car horns, or shouts during the night. City lights shone through apartment windows, and bakery smells wafted in the early hours. Those were the comforting sights and sounds of his familiar environment. The forest had an energy and cadence of its own. The night was inky black, and smells could carry for miles. The night sounds were alien and disconcerting. Grunts, growls, snapping branches, and other unidentifiable noises caused Jack to start. He couldn't judge their distance or their import. He scooted as far as he could from the entrance of the shelter and put his pack in between himself and the outdoors. Clutching his knife and his gun, his eyes would briefly close and then open wide, as he attempted to ascertain whether he was in danger.

The next morning, he was up before dawn, anxious to get to Sam. Being out in the woods alone without any amenities was highly uncomfortable, both physically and emotionally. He thought the sun would soon rise, so he sat up in his reflective bag and groaned quietly. *I'm sure I've pulled every one of my muscles.* He turned on his little heater, put on his jacket, and checked the Sun Kettle to see if the water was still warm. It was, so he made himself some instant coffee, careful to heed Roger's warning and cover it when he wasn't sipping.

Once it was light enough to see, Jack strapped on his pack and crawled out of the thicket. He scanned the woods around him, then looked at the steep path ahead of him. *I'm coming, Sam. Say a prayer for me.*

He trudged uphill until he could hardly move. He was panting with the effort, hands on his knees when he heard the crack of a branch. He couldn't tell where it came from, so he crouched beside a tree and took out his gun. He scanned the area and slowly moved toward a thicker stand of trees.

As he moved farther into the thicket, the bushes across from him rustled, and a small bunny hopped out. *Was it just a bunny?* Jack wasn't sure. But as he stood and looked around, he saw a pair of barely visible snowshoe tracks. *Should I follow them? They've been here for a while. They can't be Sam's, can they?*

He decided they were not Sam's and continued slowly upward until he came to the creek Roger had drawn on the map. He didn't know if the map was drawn to scale, but his watch said it was ten and the creek looked about halfway. *Maybe I'll make it there before dark. I hope I'm not being followed.*

After a brief rest on a boulder perched along the opposite side of the creek bed, Jack zigzagged according to the map, searching for Roger's landmarks and regularly scanning for anyone who might be following him. His fatigue grew, and his steps slowed, but he pushed himself forward, finally reaching the river that led to the waterfall and sitting on a boulder in the middle. As the water rushed along beside him, he felt he couldn't move any farther. *I'm stuck here, and someday they'll find me, a frozen statue in the middle of the river.*

Sam lay atop the waterfall, watching Jack. *What is he doing?* She carefully scanned the woods, but no one else approached. He sat there for a long time. Sam hadn't recognized him at first; he was far enough away that she couldn't make out details, and he was wearing a ski hat and sunglasses, but after watching his gait and his mannerisms from a distance, she knew.

She didn't want to give away her position, but she couldn't leave him there. She was growing anxious when he finally rose and slowly walked toward her. He left the river on the right and veered toward the slope to the waterfall. *No! If anyone is following him, we'll lose our shelter.*

Sam got up and began to run. She headed him off, and when he saw her, he smiled wide and then fell to the ground in a heap. Sam looked around, praying that no one had followed him. She slapped his face lightly with her gloved hand. "Jack," she whispered in his ear. "Jack!"

He opened his eyes. "What happened?"

"You fainted."

"No, I didn't. I don't faint. Ugh. I don't feel too good."

"Can you make it down to the cave?"

"Probably. If I can't, just give me a shove."

She smiled gently. "We need to get out of sight. Follow me down, okay?"

When they got to the cave, Sam led Jack to her woven mat in the smaller cove, helped him get his wet boots and socks off, and then dug out some dry socks. He was shivering violently, so she turned on the heater and helped him get into his reflective bag before heating water for coffee.

"Roger gave me one of those," he said weakly, pointing at the Sun Kettle.

"They're pretty handy since I can't light a fire."

"I can light one for you."

"No, the smoke would give us away, either the smoke or the light at night."

He sat up to drink the coffee when it was ready, and his shivering began to subside.

"Did you come this whole way today?" Sam asked.

"No, Roger led me to your shelter. I stayed there last night. That's amazing, by the way."

"Did Roger tell you I'd be here?"

"No. I remembered the waterfall and asked him how to get here."

Sam raised her eyebrows. "Good memory. What's going on at the camp? Is Tom okay?"

"Yes, he's fine. You didn't tell me about him." He frowned.

"I need to get back. I'm responsible for them. How can I keep them safe from here?"

"How can you keep them safe if you're dead?"

"That's what Art always says."

"I haven't met him yet. He sounds like a real pro."

"He's amazing." She smiled a little, then looked sharply at Jack. "Do you have a plan?"

He shook his head and looked into his cup.

"Why did you come all this way if you didn't have a plan?" Her brow furrowed.

"I was so afraid that something might have happened to you. I kept picturing you injured or shivering in the cold." His eyes remained on his cup. "I realize that I made a big mistake. No job is more important than you. I love you, and if you'll have me, I'll quit my job and move to Santo Milagro." He took her hands in his and looked up. "I don't want to ever lose you."

Sam's eyes and mouth turned downward, and her eyes looked moist. Her look was not what he had expected. *Why is she looking at me like that?*

"Jack," she began. Then she stopped and stared at him. "I'm married."

"What?" He jerked his hands back as if they were scalded.

"When we spoke on the phone in Vegas, you said, *You know I'll always love you, but I can't move to Santo Milagro.* I haven't seen you since last Spring. You didn't come for the holidays." She shook her head. "Tom proposed on Thanksgiving, and we got married Christmas evening, after our big holiday dinner. If you had come any of the times I invited you, this wouldn't be a surprise."

Jack's shoulders slumped. "I'm sorry. You're right. Thinking of being with you was the only thing that kept me going today. I need to sleep." He laid down, pulled the reflective blanket up to his chin, and turned to face the wall of the cave.

The campers were up early and excitedly eating pancakes and getting ready for their lesson on building shelters. Tom wanted to go too, but he could barely cross the tent. Ben and Melissa were staying with him, and David had volunteered to help with the training.

Scott puffed out his chest and said, "I don't know why you chose him. I know everything there is to know about building shelters."

"You'll be lots of help, Scott. You can teach by example, no? I bet your shelter will be amazing," Roger said. He made sure everyone had a variety of supplies, whistled for Red, and they left in high spirits. "Do any of you see a good place to make a shelter?"

David started to answer, but Roger held up his hand. "Let's use this opportunity for independent thinking and collaboration," he whispered.

"What should we think about when we pick a location?"

Sissy raised her hand and bounced up and down. "Wood we can use?"

"Wouldn't it depend on what kind of shelter we're building?" asked Lisa.

"Yes. Absolutely. And we will build several kinds today."

"If we are using a tree for support, we should find a large tree with space around it, no?" Jorge said.

"Of course," Scott said, crossing his arms and nodding sagely.

"We also need room if we're building a free-standing shelter," Sissy added.

"Two trees about six feet apart if we are using a tarp or a hammock," Lisa said.

Everyone turned and stared at her.

"What? I've been camping before."

"Why don't we start with that? Lisa, perhaps you could show everyone how to use a tarp for shelter, and then we can practice. See if you can find two suitable trees," Roger said. "Then we can discuss different ways we can use the tarp."

Lisa expertly demonstrated stringing cordage between two trees to support an A-frame tarp shelter, then David showed everyonehow they could also use a tree and stakes or a long stick to improvise.

Once everyone felt comfortable with using tarps, Roger asked for another suggestion.

"How about a shelter built against the side of a tree?" Jorge suggested. "I've seen those on YouTube."

"Do you see a good tree?"

"That one?" He pointed to an enormous pine.

"Okay. What do we need to do first?"

"Clear the ground," Scott said. "We should have done that when we set up the tarp too." He pointed at the first shelter.

"True. If we were going to sleep in our shelter, we would definitely want to clear the snow first. How do we do that?"

"I have this shovel thing in my backpack," Hailey said, holding up her e-tool.

"Excellent! We can use our entrenchment tools and our boots to remove the snow. Let's all work together on this one. It will go more quickly."

After they had cleared the snow, Roger and David showed the campers how to cut down saplings and make a shelter like Sam did further up the mountain. They each cut one and shaved off the boughs with their knives.

"We have enough materials for two, so let's split into two groups. The first step is to use leverage to lean the saplings against the tree in an A shape." Roger demonstrated on one tree, and David let the campers try it on another tree. "Then arrange the boughs on top of the frame, overlapping them like this." He continued his exposition. After they had completed their project, everyone but Hailey wanted to get inside and try it out.

"I don't want to get in there," she said. "There are probably spiders."

"Any other ideas?"

"I want to go back to camp now. I'm cold," Lisa said suddenly.

"We should stay together," Roger answered. "Is there anyone else who wants to go back?"

Everyone shook their heads.

"Please be patient, and we'll all go back together."

"No, I'm going now. I'll see you back at the tent." She turned and walked away.

Roger stared after her for a moment, then shrugged and continued the lesson. There wasn't much he could do other than return with the whole group.

"There's another kind of shelter that I like to make," said David.

"What kind is that?"

"A stand-alone, A-frame shelter made from branches."

"Good one. Can we find branches on the forest floor, so we don't have to cut too many?"

"Sure. Let's look around." He looked for an example and showed it to the rest of the group. "We'll want branches about this size or longer. We can always cut them, but they have to be fairly uniform so we can lean them against the center branch."

Once they had amassed enough branches, David showed them how to make the end supports by tying them to the center branch, then stacking the others along the sides to make a frame. "You don't have to use twine, but it makes the shelter sturdier if you do." Once the frame was completed, they wove boughs into the walls and stuffed leaves and moss into any holes they found. "The more foliage you stuff into the walls, the warmer and more weather-proof your shelter will be. Then we'll add boughs inside, too, for a softer sleeping surface."

"Great job, everyone. Thank you, David," Roger said, which earned him a round of applause from the other campers.

"Too bad we don't have time to make more so we could try sleeping out here one night," Sissy said.

Hailey shuddered. "I'm fine in the tent. My hands are sticky." She pursed her lips and wrinkled her nose.

"Ready to go back and get some lunch?" Roger asked.

"Yes!" everyone shouted.

They tromped back to camp and found Ben waiting with hot minestrone soup and grilled cheese sandwiches. "Your timing was perfect." He smiled. "And I made a lot because I figured you worked up an appetite."

"Got that right," David said. "The cold air and the exercise have me ready to eat a horse."

Once they had all collected their food and found seats at the table, Roger took a bowl and a plate to the stove. "Has Lisa made it back?"

"I haven't seen her," Ben said.

"Thanks. I'll go out and look for her after lunch. It smells great." Roger breathed in the steam rising from his soup and sighed with pleasure. The tangy smell of the tomatoes and the savory mixture of herbs made his mouth water, and grilled cheese was one of his favorites. He looked for Melissa, but she was seated between Tom and David, so he sat in an open spot next to Sissy. He found her excessive energy and constant, high-pitched stream of dialogue tiring, but he plastered a smile on his face and attempted to be polite. *She means well, but I'd rather be sitting with Melissa.* He concentrated on his meal, which was not diminished in the slightest by his chatty neighbor.

Chapter 8

After several hours of sleep Jack woke and found Sam watching him. "I'm sorry, Sam. The whole surprise revelation from your dad's journal last year really messed with my head. We are great as cousins, and we should accept that gift and treasure it. Can you forgive me?"

Of course. You're my only living relative, and I'm yours. You're important to me and I'm glad you're here."

He grinned and ran his hand through his thick black hair. "Good. Let's figure out how to capture the villain and get your survival camp back on course."

Sam smiled. "I've been thinking about how to do that, but let's have some lunch first. I'm famished."

"What do we have to eat?"

"Nothing very appetizing. We have survival food and survival food. I miss Ben's cooking."

Jack opened the food locker. "Let me see what we have. Maybe I can mix things up and make something a little different."

Jack was contemplating their options when they heard scraping in the front cave. Sam grabbed her gun and ran to the entrance of the cove, squatting there and looking around into the entrance. "Art!" She stood. "How did you find us?"

"I followed Jack." He shrugged. I stayed in the forest, observing to make sure no one else was around. "Got anything to eat?"

Jack stood as they entered, ears red. "Roger told me I'd never see you unless you wanted me to. Nice to meet you."

Art shook his hand and looked him in the eye. There weren't too many people who could do that. At six foot four, Jack was often taller than his peers.

"You did an excellent job. Roger told me you were new to traveling in the woods, especially on snowshoes, but you were vigilant and covered your tracks well."

"Thank you. That means a lot coming from you."

They nodded at each other, and Sam smiled. "Jack's trying to come up with something creative to do with those survival meals. They aren't great."

Art shrugged off his rucksack. "I have some spices. Let me see what you have."

Sam watched as the two of them conferred. By the time they had combined several dry meals and added some spice, the results were surprisingly good. They sat down together to eat.

"Remember I told you about my partner, Sam?"

"You told me a little, but mostly I got the feeling you wanted to finish my training before he returned."

Art breathed out heavily through his nose. "I will be the first person to tell you never to mix your personal life with your business life, but my partner is also my girlfriend. She's jealous of our relationship and of your business."

Sam's eyebrows rose.

"Her brother is an ex-con. He runs illegal hunting trips up here and will do absolutely anything for his little sister."

Sam's stomach dropped as she studied his face.

"Holly decided I was mentoring you for the wrong reasons and was furious when I told her you were starting your own school. She convinced her brother that they had to stop you."

"Oh, Art. Why didn't you tell me?"

"I didn't know for sure until after I talked to you on the mountain. She won't listen, though. She's a survival expert, almost as good as I am, and she is very stubborn."

"So, what should we do?"

"You're doing great. I just wanted to warn you. I'll go back down and talk to Tom when I leave you."

"Is she one of the campers?"

"I think she might be, but her brother isn't. He's likely hiding out in one of his hunting blinds."

"Do you love her?" Sam struggled to rein in her emotions.

"Yes, but I can't condone murder. I've tried to stop her. I've tried to reason with her. She warned me that if I get in the way, she'll kill me."

Sam was filled with a deep sadness. "I'm sorry, Art. I appreciate your warning."

"Do you mind if I rest here a few hours before I head back?"

"Of course not. Can I write a little note for you to take to Tom?"

"As long as it doesn't take up too much room in my rucksack." He laughed.

Sam laughed at that too. "Jack and I will take a little walk and scout out the perimeter while you rest."

"Thanks, Sam."

She pulled out some notepaper and a pen and wrote a note, then slipped it into the front pocket of Art's rucksack before donning her snowshoes and catching up with Jack outside.

Art slept through the night, so Sam and Jack gathered up branches and made a soft place to sleep in the opposite corner of the cove. Then, Sam left a lantern dimly glowing so he wouldn't be disoriented when he awoke.

Early the next morning, before the sun rose, Sam woke with a start. Art was gone. Jack was curled up against her in his reflective bag, his face partially buried with his pinched brows exposed. *I wish I could make those disappear.* She ran a finger over the deep lines but didn't wake him. She just lay there watching his face and wishing things could be different. She drifted back to sleep and woke with the sun.

Tom hadn't slept much the night before. He was worried about Sam and wondered a little about Jack, who seemed to arrive not knowing they were married.

How was it that Sam didn't tell this cousin she was so close to that she had gotten married? And since they weren't technically cousins, did they have a romantic history? He trusted Sam but wasn't quite sure if he trusted Jack. *I wish I was the one with her right now. Why did I have to get shot?* And then there was whatever was going on in the second hot tent. He knew something was going on and figured Art might be in camp, but he couldn't risk giving him away. Unable to toss and turn because of his wound, he laid still and let his mind do the tossing for him.

Sometime during the night, he saw Sissy get up and head for the tent entrance. She slid into her jacket and glanced around the tent before she let herself out. He still had trouble getting out of bed without assistance, and poor Melissa was drained. She had just recently placed a cot near his and started sleeping through the night. He listened carefully but finally fell asleep before Sissy returned.

When Tom woke to the smell of sausage, he immediately looked toward Sissy's cot to make sure she had returned safely. Relieved to see her form lying under the blankets, he relaxed and looked around the tent. No one else was around except Ben, Melissa, Jorge, and himself. He painfully pushed himself to a sitting position and gingerly made his way toward the stove. "Coffee ready yet?"

Ben smiled and poured him a cup.

"Where is everyone? Looks like more sausage for me."

"I almost guarantee they'll be back for breakfast." Ben laughed.

Stopping in for coffee, Roger said good morning, and called Red for his morning constitutional. He discovered two sets of footprints leading from the camp toward the west side of the forest, so he followed them, wondering why anyone would have gone in that direction before the sun rose. Red bounded off ahead, and his frenzied barking led Roger to a small creek, where he found Scott, frozen with a knife wound in his torso. He paused in indecision, looking in the direction of the second set of prints veering off to the left.

Clipping Red's leash to his collar, he rapidly returned to camp to get help.

"Tom," he whispered, "is there any possibility you can help me? Can you walk?"

"I can't make it very far. Can Melissa help you?"

Roger looked at Melissa. "I'm not sure. There's been a murder. Can you come?"

"It's not my forte, but I'll do what I can."

"I'm not sure who we can trust. If you think you're up for it, I would appreciate your assistance."

"Let's ask Jorge to go with us."

Roger looked around to see who else was present. Ben was at the stove, and Jorge and Sissy were sitting at the table drinking coffee. He approached Jorge and whispered in his ear. Sissy looked alarmed as Melissa and Jorge quickly donned their boots and coats. "Where are you going?"

"There's been an accident. We'll be back before breakfast," Melissa said gently before following Roger and Jorge out of the tent.

When they got to the creek, Scott's body was gone, along with the footprints Roger had seen next to the creek bed. Red ran back and forth, sniffing along the banks.

"I wasn't expecting this." Roger scratched the stubble on his cheek.

"What is it?" Melissa asked.

"There was a body in the creek and footprints in that direction." Roger pointed.

Jorge tilted his head. "Let's go in that direction and see if they start up again. Whoever was here must have walked in the creek bed."

"They might have gone in the other direction to throw us off," Melissa suggested.

"Red's faster than we are, so I can let him run ahead.

Let's walk to the left first because they might have been able to save time brushing away the footprints if they continued in the same direction." His brow furrowed. "I don't know how they could have moved the body and covered their tracks at the same time."

"Are you sure he was dead?"

Roger looked at Melissa. "He sure looked dead."

"You didn't check for breathing or a pulse?"

He shook his head, realizing his mistake. "I was trying to figure out if I should follow the footprints or go back and get help."

"It's just as well," Jorge said. "If you had waded in to check, the killer might have snuck up and got you too. If you had followed the footprints, he might have ambushed you, and if you had tried to drag the body back to camp, you would have messed up the crime scene."

"It's messed up now anyway. Let's get moving. Keep an eye out for anything that looks like it has been disturbed on either side of the creek." *I wish Tom or Jack was with us.*

Red bounded ahead but returned after a few minutes, seeming to understand what was expected of him. Roger said, "Let's try the other direction. They can't have just vanished."

They walked in silence as Red again bounded ahead. Jorge suddenly stopped and pointed. Drag marks left the creek on the other side. Roger crossed the creek and called Red, who sniffed in a circle and ran into the woods.

"I hope he doesn't get hurt," Melissa whispered.

"Me too," Roger said, listening for any unusual sounds.

They picked up their pace when they heard Red barking and found Scott behind some bushes. Footprints showed the direction the killer took, so Roger left Melissa with Scott and Red while he and Jorge followed the footprints as quickly as they could. *I should have left Jorge with her. What if the killer loops back around?*

"Don't worry," Jorge said as if reading Roger's mind. "She's armed and knows how to defend herself."

Roger nodded and pushed on through the deep snow.

"Get down," Jorge said, knocking him off his feet.

Roger felt a bullet whiz by, too close for comfort. "Roll," he said.

Rolling behind a stand of pines, they lay there for a moment catching their breath.

"There's a hunting blind up in a tree over there," Jorge indicated. "I don't know how we can flush him out, just the two of us."

"We can't just leave him. He's dangerous."

"I have a grenade."

Both men started and craned their necks to see who spoke.

"Art?" Roger asked. "How did you get here?"

"I've been following him."

"Who is he?"

"A very bad dude. He needs to be detained before he hurts anyone else. You can stay, or you can go back and help Melissa. I can take care of this guy." Art's jaw clenched, and his eyes were focused on the blind.

Roger was torn. On the one hand, he didn't want the shooter to get away. On the other, he didn't believe in taking the law into his own hands or encouraging anyone else to do so. He wished again that Tom or Jack was with them. He looked at Jorge, then back at Art. "Is there any way to do this without killing him?"

"Not that he deserves mercy, but my plan was to blow out the base of the blind so he wouldn't be able to hide there. He might break a leg if he's unlucky, but it shouldn't kill him. Shoot! There he goes. I'll go after him. Go on back to camp. I'll be there later." Art took off at a run and disappeared into the trees.

Roger and Jorge sat there for another moment, watching Art until he vanished.

"Who was that?' Jorge stood and brushed the snow off his ski pants.

"Sam's survival instructor. Let's get back to Melissa."

Sam turned on her small heater and snuggled in her reflective bag. She was warm and didn't want to leave her cozy cocoon.

Turning back toward Jack, she gave him a brief smile. "Did you sleep okay?"

"It wasn't like sleeping at the Hyatt, but it wasn't terrible." He smiled back. "At least I'm here with you. I understand what you said before about my bad timing, but there's still no one I'd rather be stranded in a cave with."

Sam sat up and put her jacket on. "We do make a good team. Did you look through your rucksack to see what Roger sent with you?"

"Not really. Art was being creative, so I let him do his thing with the survival food. Roger said he packed mostly food and water. He put the necessities on top: the reflective bag, Sun Kettle, sandwich."

"Sandwich? What sandwich?"

"Sorry. I ate it for breakfast yesterday."

"Why? I want a sandwich." Sam put on her puppy dog face, and Jack almost laughed.

"Maybe he put some other good stuff in there."

Sam's shoulders slumped. "Probably not. I am so sick of survival food. I'll go heat some water."

Jack sat up and put his jacket on while she was setting up the Sun Kettle.

She returned and did a few calisthenics while he went through his pack. "Anything good?"

"There's a small cooler box in here." An eyebrow went up as he drew out his prize.

"What? What's in it?" Sam jogged in place.

"There's a hunk of cooked steak."

Sam gasped.

"And some cooked bacon and eggs."

She held her hands out. "I'll eat them cold."

"He sent butter, rolls, and peanut butter… and some fruit."

"I love them so much! I know Ben was involved. Life is looking up."

"Let's cut off a piece of the steak and heat it up with some of the eggs and bacon."

"That sounds amazing." Sam grinned from ear to ear. "Real food. Just the thought of it is making me drool."

They put some of the food in a Sun Kettle, and Sam went out to swap it with the hot water. When she returned, she said, "Today, we should come up with a plan to catch the shooters, but let's get warmed up and have our breakfast first."

Sitting uncomfortably on her knees, with Scott's head in her lap, Melissa waited for the men to return. He was still alive, barely, but she did not know how he could survive with the massive knife wound in his torso. The person who stabbed him had removed the knife, and only the freezing temperature of the creek had kept him from bleeding to death. Melissa did her best to patch the wound and struggled to get him into her reflective bag—strenuous because Scott was unconscious, his clothes were soaked, and his breathing was ragged.

Even if they got him back to camp, Jack was away, and she didn't think she could save him. She scrubbed her hands in the snow, doing her best to remove the blood. The sharp metallic scent was so cloying she could almost taste it. The smell was nauseating, and she hoped it didn't lure unwanted predators to their location.

Quickly digging through her pack, she pulled out several instant-heating, mitten-warming packets, activated them, and stuck them in the reflective bag. Hypothermia had set in, and the bag didn't warm quickly. She kept a couple of warmers for herself.

Her hands had stiffened from the cold. Stuffing her hands in her gloves with the warmers, she waited.

"Thank goodness," she sighed as Roger and Jorge approached. "What happened?"

"Art showed up and took off after the killer. Is he still alive?" Roger nodded toward Scott.

"Just barely. I don't think he's going to make it."

Melissa looked at Scott, gently brushing his hair off his forehead. "The icy water kept him from bleeding out, but I had to get him into the reflective bag to keep him from freezing to death. Once the wound starts to thaw, I don't know what will happen. He must have extensive internal damage. He needs emergency hospital care."

"Let's try to get him back to camp. At least we can get him warm and dry, and you'll be able to see the wound better." Roger turned to Jorge. "What's the best way to transport him?"

"I guess we can hold on to the corners of the bag like a stretcher."

Roger nodded. "We can try. If that doesn't work, maybe we can put some long branches down the sides of the bag and open holes in the bottom corners. That would give us more leverage."

Melissa shrugged into her heavy pack and prepared to follow them back to camp. The first time they dropped Scott, the slick reflective bag slid from Jorge's grip. "A la verga! Lo siento, Scott. I'm going to have to take off the gloves."

"It couldn't be helped. We can remove them for a while, but at some point, our fingers will be too frozen to hold on."

"Your gloves seem to have a better grip. I'll take mine off for a while, then put them back on."

"Or we could take turns using mine. Let's try ten minutes and see how it goes."

Chapter 9

Back at camp, they laid Scott on the bed and found he had died en route. Melissa sat by his side and closed her eyes. She didn't consider herself a religious person, but she prayed to an unknown deity. *Please, bless Scott and receive him into your eternal embrace.* Roger approached her and put his hand on her shoulder. His small gesture of support somehow reinvigorated her flagging spirit. Looking up at him, she said, "How are we going to tell Hailey?"

"Tell me what?"

Melissa stiffened in surprise, her eyes widening before drooping with compassion. "Hailey. Scott was hurt out in the woods. We tried to save him, but he didn't make it."

"What? What do you mean? Where is he?"

"He's here." Melissa indicated the reflective bag next to her.

Hailey took a step back and stumbled into a chair, trembling. "What happened? Can I see him?"

"Melissa stood and pulled the reflective bag down to Scott's shoulders before moving away."

"Oh, Scott." She rushed to his side and put her forehead against his. "Is this my fault?" she whispered. Hailey turned to Melissa. "Please tell me what happened."

"We found him in a frozen creek with a knife wound. He was half frozen, and the wound was deep. We did our best to save him, but he was hurt too badly."

"Did you see who did it?"

"Roger and Jorge chased him, but I don't know if they saw his face." She looked questioningly in their direction.

"We didn't, but Art knew who he was and went after him."

"Who's Art?"

"Sam's survival instructor. He seemed to know who the attacker was and said he'll come here later."

"I feel guilty and so scared."

All four of them started when Tom asked, "Why is that?" A fleeting smile passed over his lips. He was sitting in the corner, not his usual place, and no one had noticed him.

Hailey sat next to Scott's body, her hand on the reflective bag, then looked down as she slowly began her story. "Scott and I weren't married. We were good friends, and when my husband began drinking and hurting me badly enough to put me in the hospital, he offered to run away with me. He said we could live off-grid, and Mark would never find us. We've been on the run for months, and I was finally starting to feel safe. I don't know who did this, but if it was Mark, I could be in real danger."

"Are you from this area?" Tom asked.

"No, we're from Texas."

"How would Mark have found you here?"

"I don't know. Maybe he hasn't. This just seems to be too big of a coincidence, doesn't it?"

Tom rubbed his chin.

"Based on the footprints, it looked like Scott was following the killer, who seems to be a real pro. If he realized someone was following him, he might have ambushed that person, regardless of who they were." Roger paced the tent.

Jorge nodded. "After Roger came back for help, Scott and the footprints were gone. The killer drug him along the creek bed to try to throw us off."

Tom's eyebrows narrowed. "He does sound like a pro. Was Mark in the military or into survivalism? A bush crafter?"

"No, he's a financial consultant with lots of money to throw around, though. He could have paid someone to do it."

"Since we already have someone trying to kill Sam, it might be a little farfetched to think a second person with a different motive is out here trying to kill someone else."

Hailey looked at Scott's face, and the tears came. Her face contorted, and her nose ran. She tried to say something, but she couldn't speak.

Melissa brewed a cup of tea and cautiously approached Hailey. "I've made you some calming tea, Hailey. Do you think you can drink it?"

Hailey looked up, her face red and mottled from her tears. "What's in it?"

"It's my own blend of valerian root and lavender. They are both calming herbs and completely natural."

Hailey took the cup and wrinkled her nose when she smelled it.

"The lavender is partially to help the smell. I know the valerian root is not particularly pleasant. But if you drink that and lay down for a little while, you will probably feel a lot better."

Hailey did as Melissa suggested, sipping the hot liquid. "Thank you, Melissa." She returned the cup. "I wish I could wake up and find it's just a bad dream." She walked over to her cot and laid down, pulling her blanket up over her head.

Entering the hot tent, Lisa stopped abruptly and looked around. "What's going on?"

"Shh," Melissa said, pointing toward Hailey's bed.

"Why? Is she sick?"

"Scott was killed this morning, and I've given her something to calm her."

"We need to get his body outside," Jorge said, "before we can't use this tent anymore."

"I'll help you," Roger said. "The cold will preserve the evidence for Jack."

Lisa's eyes were wide. "Who killed him? How did he die?"

"He was stabbed. We didn't catch the killer." Roger was watching her carefully, as was Tom. "Where have you been this morning?"

"I was with Ben, Sissy, and David for a while, learning how to make cordage. Ben said we'll learn how to make traps this afternoon, but…" She pointed toward Scott. "Maybe that will be postponed."

"Perhaps," Melissa said quietly. "Our numbers seem to be dwindling."

Lisa turned and left the tent without further comment.

Scott's body was heavy, so Melissa helped Roger and Jorge move it to the far side of the second hot tent.

"No one will trip over it here," Jorge said.

"We should probably remove the reflective bag, so he stays refrigerated. Maybe cover the body with a little snow, so it's not so shocking?"

"Good thinking, Melissa. We found him, so it's not quite the same as just seeing him lying here in the snow." Roger smiled. "I wonder how long it will be before Art shows up."

Melissa looked up and said, "I hope it's soon. A storm's coming, and it looks like a big one."

Roger and Jorge looked up too. The heavy gray clouds were moving rapidly, blocking out the sun, as the wind started to pick up.

Melissa shivered. "I hope Sam and Jack are okay."

Sam wanted to create a trap near the hunting blind they had discovered. It was not too far from the cave and regularly had footprints coming and going, but Jack pointed out that it was illegal to set a man trap. "We would be liable for any injuries, and possibly any trauma, despite the fact that he's trying to harm you."

"What should we do then? We could hide out near the blind and surprise him, but one of us might end up getting hurt instead."

"Art said we should stay put."

Sam sighed heavily. "I'm not very good at that."

"I know." Jack winked at her. "This is good practice for you."

She sat and thought about that for a moment, then said, "Since we're stuck out here and limited in things we can do, why don't I show you how to make some simple traps for small animals? I was going to help Roger with the lesson for camp, and you're missing all the good stuff."

"Is there a humane way to trap, or are we going to be eating what we catch?"

"The more I think about it, the more I think we should set a net trap for the shooter. We can capture him without harming him and get him back to camp. If he's actively trying to kill me, I don't think he can complain about how we catch him. Isn't a net better than a gun?"

"Maybe. Do we even have a net?"

"Not exactly, but I have camouflage tarp netting. I don't know if we could make a trap out of it, but if we can camouflage ourselves in the snow on either side of the trail, maybe one of us could toss it overhead to the other… or maybe have it on the ground with a string and pulley on either side to lift it up? I need to think on it a little."

Jack lifted an eyebrow. "Can I see the netting?"

Sam pulled her rucksack toward her and started taking things out while Jack turned on the little heater.

"It feels colder today."

"I think a storm's heading in. This might be our last chance to catch him for a few days."

"Of course, if he knows a storm's coming, he might do something rash. He won't want to sit around in the cold for several days either."

Sam pulled the netting from the depths of her bag and handed it to Jack. "It's all folded up now, but we could arrange it so one side is staked by the person throwing it. It could be thrown in such a way that it unrolls as it flies and spreads out over the shooter. Then the thrower could pull the stakes, and we could run counterclockwise and get him wrapped up in it."

"Hm." Jack thought about that. "It sounds reasonable, but I bet it won't work quite like that. We could practice on something and see what happens."

He felt along the edges of the netting and tested it for strength. "This probably wouldn't hold him for long, but if we could manage to get him tangled up in it, it would give us a few minutes at least."

"What if one or both of us were up in a tree on either side? We could put weights on the edges of the net and drop it on him, then swing down and do our tangle thing."

"Let's see how hard it is to throw this thing. If we dropped it on him, he might dodge out of the way and shoot us."

Sam drew a simple diagram. "The path to the blind is narrow, and there are trees on either side. So, what if we do something like this?" She showed Jack the diagram. "We could camouflage ourselves on either side of the trail and cut the trees loose when he stands on the net."

"This will take some time to set up, and it won't necessarily be quiet. How will we make sure he's not around?"

"Augh!" She slumped. "I don't know. I'm just throwing out ideas."

"It looks like a pretty good idea if we could get it set up and camouflage it well enough that he wouldn't notice."

"Let's go ahead and make some small traps. If the storm closes in, we might be able to cook some meat. Maybe we can cook away from the cave. That way, if we do attract attention, human or animal, we will still have a shelter to go back to."

"And if we have somewhere to hide while we're cooking, we might be able to catch a killer." Jack nodded. "So, how do we make these traps?"

Chapter 10

The woods grew darker as Sam and Jack gathered their supplies. She looked up. "I think the trap is going to have to wait. We need to get back to camp."

Jack frowned. "What about the shooter?"

"There are two of us, and if he has any sense, he's hunkering down for the storm."

They grabbed their packs and set out quickly, opting for the more direct route to save time.

By the time they reached the creek, snow had begun to fall in big, fat flakes.

"Can you keep going, or do you need to stop for lunch?"

"Can we make a brief stop? I'm exhausted."

Sam crouched down behind the rock outcrop, and he joined her. "We'll probably make better time if we refresh for a few minutes." She pulled out the rolls and peanut butter.

"Here, take a swig of this." Jack pulled out the whiskey bottle.

Sam laughed. "Priorities. Am I right?"

They each ate a couple of rolls and drank some water. Sam took a drink from the whiskey bottle and handed it back, looking up at the sky with concern. "We'd better get going. Are you okay now?"

Jack nodded. He wasn't sure why she seemed so worried, but he did his best to keep up with her. They weren't far past her shelter when the wind picked up. It was blowing from the east, so Sam tried to stay close to the trees.

As they walked, Sam said, "Why don't you tell me about your life since you left? What have you been up to?"

"It's difficult to hold a conversation while trying not to roll down the mountain."

"You can do it. It will distract you from the pain."

He stopped and pulled out the bottle again. "The truth is my life has been no different than it's always been. I ran away from you and Santo Milagro and buried myself in work. If I had free time after work, I went out with friends or colleagues. I kept myself occupied, so I couldn't think too much."

"I can't judge you too harshly for that, since I ran away to Las Vegas."

He took a swig and passed it to her.

"Liquid courage and warmer upper." Sam nodded. "Important not to have too much when we're out in the storm, though."

"There is that." He paused. "Why didn't you talk to me about what you found? Why did you just take off?"

She exhaled. "You said you would come back, and you didn't. You didn't even call or write. By the time I found the journals, I knew you weren't going to move to Santo Milagro. I didn't want what I found to influence your decision."

"But why did you leave?"

"I was running away from my thoughts and feelings, but I realized they followed me wherever I went. I was bored and lonely at home. It wasn't just about you; it was how I felt when you were around and the enormous void when you left."

"I felt rejected when I got to your house and read your note. I believed that you were the one person in my life who was safe, the one person who would never hurt me."

Sam could feel him pulling away and shrinking into himself, so she reached out and put her hand on his sleeve. She waited until he looked at her. "I wasn't rejecting you; I was trying to protect myself."

"So, tell me about Tom. I can't believe you got married and didn't tell me." He bent over and put his hands on his knees. "Hold on a sec. I need to catch my breath." After a couple of seconds, he said, "Okay. Let's go."

"I was getting close to him but kept thinking about you. I even got a tattoo of you and me while I was in Vegas."

"You did? Let me see."

"It's too cold. It's on my right shoulder. I'll show you at camp. Anyway, when we talked on the phone, and you told me that you could never give up your job and move to Santo Milagro, I finally let go. I didn't think Tom was the man God intended for me, so I was prepared to come home alone, but as I was getting ready to leave, it felt so wrong." Sam stopped and put her finger to her lips. "Shh. Did you hear something?" she whispered.

Jack shook his head, so Sam threw a large rock at a nearby tree and waited.

"Okay. Let's keep walking. On the morning I left, Tom drove into the parking garage and told me he was coming with me if that was alright. And it was. Suddenly a weight lifted, and I was glad he was there. He helped me find a new purpose in life and found Art for me."

"Then, he proposed at Thanksgiving."

"Yes." Sam smiled. He was there when I was mourning the loss of my pet turkey and cheered me up when you canceled. He applied for a job with the Sheriff's department in Santo Milagro and gave up his busy job in Vegas."

"And you got married on Christmas." Jack's eyes looked suspiciously damp.

"We went to the church with all our friends and Tom's family after Christmas dinner. The pipe organ played carols, and everyone was dressed up for the holiday. It was beautiful."

"And you love him?"

Sam could see the question he was asking in his eyes. More than me?

"I love him very much. Not the way I love you because blood or not, we're family, but yes, I love him."

Jack nodded slowly. "If I were to ever love anyone enough to marry them, it would be you, but I'm glad you're happy, and I'm glad we're still family. I might be able to like Tom once I stop being mad at him."

Sam punched him lightly in the arm and handed him the bottle. She looked back and saw someone standing in a shooting stance in the distance. Grabbing Jack's sleeve, she yanked him to the ground. "Get behind the tree," she said, pulling out her own rifle. She felt a bullet pass by, so aiming carefully, she shot in the shooter's direction. The wind was strong, and the bullet went wide. She tried again and saw the man fall.

"What happened?"

"I hit him. Now, I don't know what to do. We need to get back to camp and get help. It's dangerous to be out in this weather. We could get disoriented or worse. We need Roger." She rummaged in her pockets and found a large red ribbon, which she tied securely around a branch. "Come on. Hurry. I don't know how badly he's hurt."

"It's a man?"

"I don't know. Maybe. We're not far from camp."

They ran and walked toward camp, finally arriving out of breath. The smell of food was so tantalizing, but something had to be done. Jack peeked his head in the tent and got Ben's attention. "Can you send Roger out? And save us some food. Please."

"You and Sam?"

Jack nodded. "Send Roger to the second tent, please. It's an emergency."

Sam and Jack entered the second tent, only to find Art sitting on Jack's cot.

"Art?"

"Sam." He smiled. "I had to find some shelter. This weather is intense."

Roger entered the tent and hugged Sam.

"Guys, I shot someone not too far from here. He was shooting at us, and I returned fire. He fell, but I don't know how badly he's hurt. Maybe I should have checked on him first, but I was worried about getting disoriented or ambushed. Can you help us check on him?"

Roger looked at Art. "I'm sorry, man. It looks like one more time out in the cold before dinner. We can take Red too. He's a good tracker."

"Yep." Art stood and put his jacket on. "Let's go. At least I got to thaw for a few minutes. Dinner when we return."

Sam led them to her marker, adding additional markers along the way. When they arrived, she pointed toward the place where the person was standing. The four of them spread out and carefully approached the area, but the shooter was gone.

"It's snowing hard, but I can see the depressions where he was standing and where he fell. There's a little blood here." Roger reached down with his gloved hand. "We could follow his tracks for a while until the wind and snow have erased them completely, but it looks like he's mobile and doesn't want to be found."

"I hope he'll be okay." Sam's brow furrowed.

"Sam, he shot at you. He ran away. He is probably the person who killed Scott," Roger reasoned.

"What! Someone killed Scott?"

"Let's get back," Art said. "You can hear all about it over dinner."

They all tromped back to the second tent. Roger went to get them some dinner, and Red curled up in front of the stove.

When Roger returned with three plates of food, Art accepted his plate and said, "Thank you. This looks great." Ben had dished him out a large helping of steak, mashed potatoes, and broccoli. "I've been outdoors since the day Tom was shot, and this is the first warm meal I've had, except for that delicious survival food." He winked at Sam.

"You should have come to us sooner," Roger said.

"I'm worried that if the shooter sees me, I'll be putting myself and everyone else in danger."

"Tell me about Scott." Sam took a big bite of juicy steak and almost lost her train of thought.

The mouthwatering aroma combined with the rich taste of beef and the perfectly cooked, tender chew threatened to overwhelm her deprived senses.

"Are you okay?" Jack waved his hand in front of her face and laughed. "She has been craving real food, and on her first day back, she gets steak." He snapped his fingers.

Sam blinked. "Scott. What happened? This is so good."

Roger shared the story of finding Scott in the creek, returning for help, then finding the body and the footprints missing.

"I didn't know about that part," Art said, around his mashed potatoes.

"You said you were following him. I figured you saw what happened."

"I was actually staking out the blind, waiting for him."

"When we were trying to figure out which way he went and where he left the creek, I saw one small footprint near the side of the creek-side path. I don't know who it belonged to or how it got there, but it wasn't the killer's print. He might have wiped away someone else's tracks along with his own. I'm not sure."

"What happened when you discovered which way he had gone?" Jack asked.

"I sent Red on ahead, and he found Scott. Then, Melissa stayed with him while Jorge and I pursued the killer." He continued the story with Art showing up and Jorge and himself returning to help Melissa get Scott back to camp.

"What happened when you followed the killer?" Sam asked Art.

"I chased him, but he has dozens of blinds and other hiding places out here. He's the only person more difficult to find than I am."

"You saw him, though; you saw his face? You know who it was?"

"I didn't see his face, but I know it was him."

Sam stared at him. "Who?"

"Holly's brother."

"How do you know it was him?"

"He's the only other person out here."

"You can't know that. There could be hikers, campers, hunters."

"Trust me, Sam. It's him."

She shrugged and let it go. "What happened when you got Scott back to camp?"

Roger shook his head, his eyes down. "He didn't make it. The only thing that kept him alive was the freezing water, and when Melissa tried to stave off the hypothermia by getting him into the reflective bag, he bled to death. The wound was bad. Even if we'd been able to get him to an ER immediately, he probably wouldn't have made it."

"How's Hailey handling it?"

"At first, she said it might be her fault and that she was afraid. She told us that she wasn't really married to Scott. He invited her to live off grid with him when her husband got so abusive, he was putting her in the hospital. She thought maybe her husband killed Scott." Then his death seemed to register, and she broke down completely. Melissa gave her some calming tea and had her lay down."

"Poor thing."

"Can you describe Hailey for me?" Art asked.

Roger thought about it. "She's short, maybe five foot three. She has very long, red hair, the color of Sam's, and lots of facial piercings: eyebrows, nose, lip, tongue, ears, she practically glows when the sun hits her."

"What do the other female campers look like?"

"Sissy is a little taller than Hailey; very slender, with long, black hair."

"I sort of know Sissy," Jack said. "She has been stalking me for about six months and always seems to know where I'll be. I was ready to turn around and leave when I saw her here, but my ride was gone."

"Poor Jack." Sam patted his knee before going back to eating her steak.

"Lisa is taller, maybe five eight, with short blonde hair and blue eyes. She's a lot of trouble."

Art nodded. "Thank you."

"How are you connected to our female camper?"

"She's my business partner and girlfriend, I'm ashamed to say. She wants Sam and her survival camp out of the way and told me she'd kill me if I intervened. I must stop her."

"You don't want to tell us who she is?"

"She's very dangerous. I don't want anyone in camp trying to get in her way. I'll follow her when she leaves to meet her brother."

Roger frowned. "Don't you think it might be better if we were forewarned? We could possibly defend ourselves if something happens?"

"No, she thinks she's safe right now and won't hurt anyone. Just make sure she doesn't know I'm here."

"Roger, I'd like to examine Scott's body after dinner if you could lead the way. We'll need a good flashlight."

Roger looked at Jack with a frown. "Are you sure you don't want to wait until morning? It's howling out there."

"We might take another look in the morning, but I think it's best to do an initial exam as soon as possible. The longer we wait, the more likelihood of contamination." Jack set his empty plate aside.

Roger nodded and grabbed a flashlight and a lantern.

"Did you take any photos before you took him outside?"

"No, sorry. Most of our phones are dead, and I don't think anyone has a camera." He led Jack outside and around the side of the tent. They bent forward, pushing against the wind, blinded by the snow. They turned the corner and stopped. "We covered him partially with snow so he wouldn't shock everyone, and without any protection from the wind on this side, it looks like he's turned into a snow drift."

Jack stood and stared at the mound of icy snow. "I wish you had put down a tarp or something. This is going to be difficult."

"I'm sorry, Jack. We weren't expecting this storm, and none of us really knew what we were doing. I don't know how many times I wished you or Tom were with us."

"It's not your fault. I understand, but how do we fix this? Did anyone take any notes or make any observations that can help? Can we partially thaw the ice and put a tarp over him until tomorrow? I don't have any experience in this type of situation."

"I guess we could bring a little propane heater out here to thaw the ice."

"Let's try that then. Maybe we can dig a little once it's loosened up." Jack's brow furrowed in thought. "As long as we don't dig too deep and destroy the evidence."

"Could I suggest that we wait until morning? Whatever we do tonight will be frozen over again in the morning, no?"

"Yes. Okay. We'll wait."

They went back inside to find Art in one of the cots, facing the tent wall with his covers pulled up over his head. Ben was retrieving the dishes. He reported that the folks in the first tent were getting ready for bed. David and Jorge entered behind him and began to exclaim how wonderful it was to see Sam again.

She smiled and put a finger to her lips. "You guys go ahead and get comfortable; I need to go see Tom."

Everyone was settling in for the night when Sam tiptoed toward Tom's cot and kissed him on the cheek. His eyes flew open, and he grinned happily. "What a sight for sore eyes." He reached for her.

"Shh. Don't make a spectacle, or we'll never get to bed. Can I sleep with you there?"

"You had better. Could you sleep in the front, though? It's better if nothing unexpected touches my back."

She knelt in front of his cot. "I am so glad you got lucky. Everyone says you did. I was very worried."

"Give me a kiss and crawl under these covers. I need a snuggle."

Melissa stayed where she was but smiled to see her friends reunited at last.

78

Chapter 11

The storm raged through the night, and Roger lay with his eyes open. Red slept under his bed. The only thing he was sure of was that Art slept hard and snored like a locomotive. If it wasn't for the gusting wind, he might have feared that the mystery camper would recognize the snore. When dawn broke, Roger was exhausted but got up to put more wood on the fire and make coffee. Ben was getting ready to leave for the first tent to make breakfast.

"Ben, can I talk to you for a minute before you go?" Roger whispered.

"What's going on?"

Roger explained about Art and the mystery camper. "If you see someone leave, let me know, and please don't tell anyone about our visitor."

"Got it. I'll bring my breakfast in here to eat and bring him some too."

"Thanks. She'll probably head out as soon as the storm lets up, and Art will follow. Jack and I are going to try to thaw the mound of ice covering Scott's body so he can examine it. You'll save us some breakfast, no?"

"Absolutely. Have fun out there." Ben grinned.

Jack woke to Roger shaking his arm and calling his name. "Get your boots on, Jack. It's time to go dig in the snow."

He sat up and began putting said boots on. "Where's the coffee?"

"I thought you might ask me that. Here." Roger handed him a cup.

"I'm going to take the portable heater out there, but I need to keep an eye on it, so come on out once you finish that."

Jack bundled up and drank his coffee, then joined Roger outside, whacking his hands together and stomping his boots.

"It's starting to thaw around the edges, huh."

"Just try not to thaw the body. That could get ugly. I just want to examine the wound."

"When the cap of ice thaws, we can dig with those trowels."

"Or our hands when we get close."

Roger made a face, then picked up a trowel to assess the hardness. "I think we might be able to chip away at it now as it gets softer. We don't want it too soft."

As they got closer and the snow got softer, Jack began brushing it off with his gloved hands, concentrating on the torso. "Here we go," he said softly. I don't want to disturb the wound." He finally got an unobstructed view of the damage and sat back on his heels. "The killer really meant business. This is ugly."

Roger swallowed hard. He had seen the fresh wound, but he had forgotten how grisly it was. "When we found him, we were more concerned with keeping him alive than what this looked like. It's like something out of a horror movie, huh."

Jack took off his snow gloves and pulled on a pair of medical gloves before examining the wound more closely. "It looks like the killer used a survival knife with a serrated edge. The exact size is difficult to determine anyways, without testing, but when he twisted the knife, he made it even more difficult. If we find a discarded knife, we can submit it for testing. Do we have a tarp we can use to cover the body for now to protect it against more snow drifts and ice?"

Roger nodded and backed away. "I'll be right back."

"Anyone ready for breakfast?" Ben's booming voice rang out. Everyone lined up for a plate filled with frittata, sausage, and pancakes.

Tom was sitting at the table, and Sam had disappeared, so Melissa took him a plate and asked if he'd like more coffee.

"Thank you for everything, Melissa. I think I'll owe you for life." He smiled.

"You just keep making Sam happy, and we're even." She went to get him more coffee, then sat down with him to enjoy breakfast.

"Ben, you're the best cook ever," Sissy said.

"Here here," David called out.

"Thanks, everyone. I love an appreciative audience."

"I hate to be Dudley downer," Roger stood between the table and the stove, "but due to the weather, we're going to have to do things indoors today. You can read or play board games, and this afternoon, we can have a lesson on building traps, although it will have to be somewhat theoretical."

"I think we should get a refund," Lisa said. "This camp has not met expectations."

Roger eyed her frowning face. "You might be able to get a partial refund, but your food alone was almost worth the cost of the camp; plus, whether you attended or not, most of the scheduled classes have been held. Crime and weather are not something we could have foreseen."

The other campers nodded, and Lisa frowned harder. Suddenly everyone grew silent as Hailey walked past the table like a ghost, pallid face and red-rimmed eyes, her long red hair tangled and floating behind her. She quietly took a plate and handed it to Ben.

"How hungry are you?" Ben asked quietly.

"Pretty hungry."

"Coffee?"

"Yes, please."

Melissa got up to help her carry her breakfast to the table and made a place for her next to Tom.

Ben took his breakfast to the second tent, leaving Roger near the stove. "Melissa, could you help me a moment?" he called.

When she approached, he said, "Act like you're helping me make coffee, okay?"

While they played out their pantomime, Roger whispered, "Once everyone gets involved playing games or whatever, could you suggest to Tom that since he's getting stronger, maybe you two should try taking a short walk? You can help him with his jacket and take him to the other tent so he can talk to Art. He will want to do that."

"Can you shovel a little path?"

"I think I can manage."

"I'll do my part then."

When she was reseated, Roger grabbed a couple more plates, and Melissa resumed eating her then-cold breakfast. "I was thinking, Tom," she said quietly, "since you're doing so much better, maybe we should try taking a little walk outside."

"Isn't it…"

"Roger said he'd shovel us a little path so you can walk a short distance without pulling out your stitches." She winked at him.

Tom nodded. "That sounds great. I haven't been outside in days."

Everyone else cleaned their dishes and broke into groups to play games or individually to read or chat. Melissa cleaned her and Tom's dishes and helped him into his boots and his jacket. She helped him out of the tent door and along the path Roger had shoveled to the second tent. He leaned on her as they walked blindly into the wall of wind and snow.

Opening the flap of the second tent, they stepped inside to find Ben, Art, Sam, and Jack finishing their breakfasts.

"Hey, Tom, glad you could make it." Art's eyes crinkled, but his expression otherwise remained neutral.

"This is my first time out of my cave."

"Are you doing better?"

"I'm getting there. What's going on?" Melissa helped him out of his jacket and got a chair for him to perch on.

"According to Sam's schedule, we should be picked up tomorrow, but the storm probably shut everything down. Ben said we're starting to run low on food, not critically low, but we won't make it more than a few days."

"They'll probably get here as soon as they can. I expect Holly will make a move this afternoon. I'll be ready."

"Do you need backup? Roger can probably go with you if you need help."

"I'll be okay. I just need to find her brother. I don't think Holly will harm me, but he's a killer."

"If anyone makes a move to leave the tent, I'll call out, so you'll know. Are you sure you don't want assistance?"

"No, I just wanted to make sure you know what my intentions are. That way, if something goes wrong, you can inform the authorities... being yourself."

Tom chuckled. "I haven't been sworn in quite yet, but I'll inform myself once I am. Be careful out there, Art."

"I will. Thanks, Tom." They shook hands, and Tom rose from his chair. "How long are you going to hide out in here?" he asked Sam. "I want you in the lion's den with me."

"I'll be in shortly. Give me a kiss." Tom happily obliged.

"When the rest of you join us, I think we should ask the campers about their whereabouts when Scott was killed. I don't want to assume that our scenario is fact. We need to follow procedure and interview our suspects."

"We'll be there soon," Jack said.

Melissa helped Tom with his jacket, and the wind pushed them the short distance back to the first tent.

"All of the campers are pretty suspicious about whatever's going on over here," Ben said. "If you and Jack come over there with us, they'll assume that they know what's been going on."

"Plus, we can get more coffee."

"How did you even survive in the wild?" Ben laughed.

"It was rough, let me tell you. We need to invent some instant-heat espresso packets. I'm sure we'll all be millionaires. No one should have to survive without their caffeine."

"Will you be okay over here?" Jack asked Art.

"Of course. It's like being in the woods, except I have warmth and a soft place to sit."

They all smiled.

"Let's get over there and let our presence be known, then. Ready?"

Sam and Roger nodded. They put their jackets on and waved to Art on their way out.

When Roger entered the tent with Sam and Jack, there was complete silence before the pandemonium hit. Everyone got up and spoke at once.

"Sam, you're okay."

"Jack, where have you been?"

"When did you guys get back?"

Sam was overwhelmed but walked over to Tom and hugged him. "We're here now," she whispered.

Jack, lacking the same safeguard, smiled and told everyone he was glad to be back.

"What are you all up to on this stormy day?" Sam asked.

"Lisa was just telling us why she thought she should get a refund," Sissy said.

"Aren't you all enjoying being part of a real-life mystery story?"

"I am," David said, "and I know who did it."

"Would you like to tell us?"

"No, actually, I'd like to speak to Tom in private."

Sam's eyebrows rose. "In that case, I'll give you some space and go find some more coffee." She walked over to the stove and was happy to see a pot of coffee waiting for her.

Melissa approached and gave her a hug. "I'm sure glad you're back. I was worried."

"I was fine but getting sick of survival food.

Also, I have a little scratch from an arrow that you could look at if you're so inclined."

"Is it infected?"

"It wasn't the last time I looked, but it has pulled open a couple of times."

"Jack gave Tom stitches. He was very brave."

"Who? Tom or Jack?"

Melissa giggled. "Both, I think."

Sam sat on Tom's cot, and Melissa went to get Jack. Tom lips thinned as Jack approached Sam. She took off her jacket and her shirt sleeve and let him unwrap the bandage on her arm.

"Are you listening to me?" David demanded.

"No. Wait a minute, please."

Jack unwrapped the bloody bandage to reveal a large, raw wound. He prodded the wound as he was speaking to Sam. She made a grimace but didn't cry out or make any other indication that she was in pain.

Tom struggled to stand and walked over to the cot. "Why didn't you tell me you were injured?"

"If you want to know the truth, I completely forgot about it. It happened on the day that you got shot, and I've mostly ignored it. I rolled on it once and almost screamed, and I unwrapped it to clean it once and saw that it had reopened, but mostly it has just been a fact of life."

"You were laying on it last night. I had no idea."

"Jack says it needs some stitches. Any advice?" Sam smiled at him. "I hear you were very brave."

Tom shuddered. "Can't she wait and get that done at the hospital with some local anesthetic?"

"No, I take special pleasure in torturing my cousin." Jack chuckled.

Tom looked like he was about to erupt.

"He's just kidding, Tom. He told me I could wait."

Sam put her hand on his cheek and smiled.

"At some point, we're going to have to bury the hatchet, detective. We're family now."

Tom looked at Jack's smiling face, and he wanted to punch him. *I'm usually an easy going guy. Why does Jack bring out the worst in me? Just the sight of him makes me feel violent.*

"Let me finish wrapping up Sam's wound, then we'll talk, okay?" Jack looked at him kindly. "We should clear the air."

Tom nodded and went back to his chair, where David was waiting impatiently.

He sat and said, "David, I understand that you want to be heard, but I'm having my own personal crises here, so please try not to provoke me right now."

"Sorry. I'm not trying to provoke. Just listen, okay? There's something wrong with Hailey. She wasn't around the morning Scott was stabbed, and her reaction when she found out wasn't normal. I think she had something to do with it."

"Were you here when she found out? I didn't hear your name mentioned."

"I was outside. I came in when she was talking about her husband."

"Thank you for letting me know. I'll keep it in mind."

"You don't believe me."

"It's not that I don't believe you; it's that I have eyewitness accounts of the person who killed him, and they don't match."

"Well, keep an eye on her because something isn't right."

"Okay. Thank you." Tom nodded.

After Jack finished patching up Sam's arm, he approached Tom with his jacket. "Let's go over to the other tent and talk for a few, okay?"

Tom nodded and allowed Jack to help him with the jacket. Stepping outside the tent was akin to diving headfirst into a snowy hurricane. The wind blew in gusts, filling eyes and nose with snow.

The twelve-foot walk seemed to take an eternity as they bent against the onslaught.

Tom was panting by the time they entered the second tent. Art was gone, so they had the space to themselves. Jack helped Tom remove his jacket and sat down on his cot. Tom looked around. "You can sit here too if you like."

He sat down gingerly and looked at Jack.

"I'll admit," Jack began, "that when I arrived and found out Sam was alone on the mountain and that you two had gotten close, I was jealous, and I intended to win her back."

Tom studied him.

"But when I found her, she told me you were married and that she loved you. She pointed out that I had said I couldn't leave my job and didn't come to any of the family events or even talk to her for months. I haven't been a good cousin or a good friend."

"I was surprised she hadn't told you we were married."

"I was surprised, too, but I realized I had made myself unavailable. I disappointed her over and over again."

"Why?"

Jack shrugged. "Sam and I both have trust issues. Both of us had loved ones leave us, although unwillingly. We both thought we were safe together, that neither one of us would hurt the other."

Tom shifted a little on the cot.

"When Sam found her dad's journal that said we weren't blood relations, she left me a note and the journal and fled to Vegas. I arrived at the ranch to find her gone. We both had our reasons, but I felt betrayed. I felt like she wasn't the safe person I thought she was."

"So why did she leave?"

"I had told her I would think about moving to Santo Milagro, but I didn't call or write. I was silent for weeks. She told me that by the time she found the journals, she knew I wasn't coming, and she didn't want it to affect my decision."

"Can I ask you something?"

"Sure."

"Were you and Sam ever romantically involved?"

"You never asked her that?"

"No, it didn't matter, except when you two were away from camp, I started to wonder."

"We have never been romantically involved, except maybe in my fantasies." Jack smiled. "We've never even kissed."

Tom nodded. "That makes me want to punch you less."

Jack laughed. "I love Sam, and she loves me too, but as cousins. We've never been anything else. We're like peas in a pod, so much alike even though we grew up in completely different circumstances. Sometimes I know what she's thinking even before she says it."

"Thank you, Jack. She has always talked about you so much, and she got that tattoo. Once, in Vegas, I asked her if she would marry you if you moved to Santo Milagro and asked her. She said, 'I don't know. Probably not at this point since we're not really in that place, but it's not relevant since he can't give up his job.'"

"Way to kick a guy when he's down, Tom." Jack looked distraught.

"I'm sorry. That's not how I meant it. I just wanted you to understand why I was so worried. I've never really understood your relationship, and I was hoping she wasn't going to leave me once you reappeared."

"Not a chance. She told me in no uncertain terms that she's with you, and I'm her cousin. Now, let me help you get that jacket back on, and we'll rejoin the party next door."

"Thank you for sorting things out between us. I appreciate it."

"You're welcome. I *must* get a look at that tattoo."

"At least it's somewhere decent." Tom smiled.

"Ready to brave the storm?"

"Yep." Jack opened the flap. "Nope," he said as the wind pushed him to the door of the first tent.

Everyone played games until lunch time when they took a break and ate build-your-own hoagies and leftover rabbit stew.

Tom enjoyed watching Sam eat. Her enjoyment was self-evident. "You must have really suffered out there in the wild," he whispered.

"Oh, Tom, being constantly cold and having to subsist on survival food was the absolute worst. I am so happy to be warm and have something delicious to eat. The only thing better would be a nice, hot bath."

"We'll take care of that when we get home."

"That sounds heavenly. I'll dream about it tonight. Did you and Jack talk things out?"

"Yes, he's a pretty decent guy."

Sam smiled. "He is."

When lunch was coming to an end, Roger said, "As promised, we'll have a lesson on traps this afternoon. It won't be quite the same as going outdoors and setting them, but it will give you a basic understanding of how they are built and how they work. We'll use the table, but if you don't want to participate, you can retire to your cot or a chair and do whatever you like."

As usual, Lisa decided to leave the tent after lunch. When she left, Tom called out to her. "Hey, Lisa, has the storm let up?"

She looked up and shrugged. "A little."

"Be careful out there, okay?"

She ignored him.

"Lisa!" He didn't care if she heard him. He just wanted to make sure that Art knew she was leaving if he had returned.

"Before Roger begins your afternoon lesson, Tom would like to question you all about your whereabouts when Scott was killed. No one was in the tent, so if you could all just give a brief statement, it would help him get a picture of what everyone was doing at the time." Sam sat down next to him and let him take over.

"Why should we have to give him a statement?" Sissy asked.

"He's a police detective, so when the authorities arrive, he'll be the person they refer to."

"Why don't we start with you, Sissy?" Tom suggested.

"I was with Ben, Mark, and Lisa, learning how to make cordage."

"Ben, did you start your cordage lesson before you made breakfast?"

"No, sir. We went out after breakfast."

"So, where did you go before breakfast?"

"Just out for a walk."

"Alone?"

"Yes."

"You are ignoring the buddy system?"

"My buddy was unavailable."

Roger said, "When I came back for help, you were both sitting right here drinking coffee."

"Whatever." She got up and left the table.

"David?"

"I got up a little late and went out to the loo. I arrived just after you guys got back."

Tom nodded.

"Hailey?"

"I was sleeping."

"You weren't here when I came back for help," Roger interjected.

"I don't know, then. Maybe I was using the restroom." She sat on her cot, looking vague and trying to brush the mass of tangles from her hair.

Sam felt sorry for Tom. His shoulders slumped, and he looked very tired.

"If at least a couple of you upheld the buddy system, you would have alibis. As it is, there's not one alibi among the lot of you. I hope you all trust each other."

They looked at each other suspiciously, and Sam had to head toward the stove to hide her smirk.

Chapter 12

Roger set up materials for several different traps on the table, and everyone gathered around. "The type of trap we make depends on what we are trying to catch. The first type of trap is called a deep hole trap. For this type of trap, you don't need any extra supplies. You dig a deep hole, sometimes wider at the bottom, and sometimes with a slightly elevated cover that small animals can try to hide under."

"What kind of animals can that trap?" David asked.

"Frogs, snakes, and rats."

"Eee, who would want to eat those?"

"You'd be astonished at what you would be willing to eat if you were starving. If you want to get a little fancier, you can make a snare trap. You can do this by using a wire or a piece of paracord. Start by making figure-eight knots on each side of your cord. Does anyone know how to do that?"

David raised his hand.

"Go ahead and demonstrate for us, David."

He took the paracord from Roger and showed the others how to double the cord and make a loop, then pass the doubled cord through the loop to make a knot.

"Great. Thank you, David. Now we have two figure eight knots, and we're going to pass one through the other to make a snare. We'll have to wait for the weather to improve so we can find good animal trails where we can place our snares, but basically, we secure one end of the snare to a post or branch and hang it where an animal of the appropriate size will pass through and get caught. Why don't all of you see if you can make a snare using a figure-eight knot?"

Tom, who was less interested in traps than he was in his bride, put his arms around Sam and nuzzled her ear. "I wish we had a little privacy," he whispered.

"Our rescuers should be coming soon," she whispered back. "I am having second thoughts about this endeavor."

"This has been a rough trial run, but it won't always be like this. Don't give up."

Sam leaned her head against his shoulder. "I love that you're so supportive, even when you've been injured."

Jack eyed them from the other side of the table, and Sissy scrutinized Jack from her chair in between.

"We'll try one more, and then we'll call it a day. The third type of trap is called a deadfall, and the best one, in my opinion, is called the Paiute deadfall. We need a large flat rock or log, a diagonal stick to support the weight, another shorter stick to hold up the diagonal stick, a small twig for the trigger, and a small piece of wood for the toggle. Start with the large stick, about the width of your thumb. We'll carve a notch near the bottom for the cordage, and near the top, for the shorter stick. The toggle will also have a notch for the cordage and will be wrapped around the larger stick." Roger was demonstrating all of this and assisting the campers.

Jack, fascinated, didn't notice Sissy moving closer to where he was sitting. When she leaned against him, he flinched and bumped the table, causing everyone's projects to fall.

"Hey!" David said.

Jack moved away from Sissy as if she had scalded him and Sam stood. "Sissy, please be considerate of other people's personal space. Jack, could you come help me get the fire ready for dinner?"

"Do we have to do something special for dinner?" he asked when they approached the stove.

"No, I was just trying to rescue you."

"Thank you. I don't know what her problem is."

"Some people just don't have boundaries. We'll be out of here soon."

"I certainly hope so. The cave was better."

Ben entered the tent and meandered over to where they were standing. "Everything okay?"

"Yes, I was just showing Jack how to prepare the stove for dinner." Sam winked. "He needed to get away from the table."

"Ah. Would you like some additional dinner duties, sir?"

"Yes, please."

Sam returned to the table, where Roger was finishing up his lesson. "Great job, everyone. Why don't you relax for a few minutes while our master chef whips up some dinner?" He gathered up his supplies and sat down with Sam and Tom.

"I think everyone enjoyed that, Roger. Too bad we couldn't have included the out-door aspect with some tracking, but you made the lesson very informative anyway."

"Thanks, Sam. I did my best. How're you doing, Tom? You've been up and about for a long time."

"I'm a little sore, but I'm happy that Sam's here with me." His eyes twinkled in the happy way Sam liked to see.

"I'm so thoughtless. Would you like to lay down for a little while?"

"Nope. We can just go to bed early." He smiled. "And we can sleep with our heads in the opposite direction, so you don't have to sleep on your sore arm."

Lisa returned just as dinner was ready, shrugged off her jacket, and joined everyone in line. Ben served spaghetti and surreptitiously gave Roger a plate to take next door. He stood and chatted with Ben until everyone had been seated, then slid outside unnoticed.

Art was laying on his cot, warm and dry. "You didn't follow Lisa?" Roger asked.

"Spaghetti? Yum." Art reached for the plate.

Roger scratched his whiskers. "I have to get back."

Art nodded without looking up. "Thanks." He took a big bite.

When Roger returned to the first tent, he caught Hailey watching him. She was sitting at the end of the table, picking at her food. Her red-rimmed eyes and her tangled hair gave her a slightly wild look. *She's been through a lot.*

Roger got another plate and sat next to Melissa. She was a slow eater, so he caught up in no time. She looked at him, then glanced at Lisa. "What do you think about that?" she asked under her breath.

"I'm not sure. The weather hasn't let up. It's ferocious out there."

"Anyone up for some cards?" Jorge asked. "Tom won all the jerky, so we'll have to decide on some new stakes."

"I'll return your jerky so I can win it back again." Tom laughed.

"I'm in," Sam said. "Let's clear the table first."

Everyone began clearing their dishes and settled at the table for a game, except Hailey, who laid on her cot and pulled her blankets over her head.

They started with blackjack, then moved to five-card draw. Lisa was the big winner and smiled for the first time in a week. "Sorry, everyone, it's time for me to hit the hay."

She was heartily congratulated on her card skills as the party began to break up. David frowned but didn't say anything. The men left for the second tent, and he skulked around outside, watching Lisa when she left to use the outhouse, then finally going inside to get ready for bed.

"What are you doing?" Roger asked.

"I don't trust her. She's up to something."

"You don't trust Hailey either."

"Yeah. It's hard to watch everyone at once."

"True. Let's get some sleep. Maybe the storm will let up tomorrow. I think everyone's getting cabin fever."

Like the previous night, Roger fell asleep to the sound of wind and snoring but woke suddenly when he was hit with a gust of frigid air. He sat up and listened. The snoring had stopped.

Glancing around the tent, he noticed that David and Art were both missing.

Assuming they had either gone to use the outhouse, or in Art's case, who knew, he rolled over and went back to sleep.

The next morning, he awoke to screaming. He pulled on his boots and his jacket and joined Sam and Jack outside. Sissy was sitting in the snow outside the outhouse screaming her lungs out. It was easy to see that she had tripped over a large body lying face down between the tents. Sam was trying to calm her, and Jack was examining the body.

"Try to keep everyone back, Roger." Jack looked up. "It's Art."

"Is he…"

"Yes, at least two hours, although the temperature makes it difficult to be accurate."

"It might be easier to tell by the drifting. The wind has been howling all night. I woke up at one point and noticed he and David were gone. David might be able to tell us what time that was."

"David's missing. I'll finish up here and take some photos, then we should move him over by Scott. Can you inspect these footprints and see if you can make sense of them?" Jack indicated a mass of different-sized boot and snowshoe prints. "The wind is obliterating them."

Roger looked at Sissy's fresh prints, then compared them to the others. The main difficulty, other than the wind and snow, was the location. Almost everyone had gone back and forth to the outhouse, and the tracks were a jumbled mess. Art's footprints were the largest and most identifiable. They were partially protected from the wind as they passed between the tents. Several other footprints went back and forth between the tents. A larger set of prints left the forest and returned. Finally, one additional set of prints followed the first set into the forest.

"I'm going to follow the tracks going into the forest. Jorge, can you join me?" Roger whistled for Red and started carefully moving forward. Jorge grabbed a rifle and jogged to catch up.

Sam took Sissy inside and left her with Melissa. When she returned to where Jack was working, he stood and shook his head. "Very strange," he said. "Another stabbing, but not by the same person. A strong blow with a downward trajectory, right between his shoulder blades. He was my height. He fell forward, and there were small, deep footprints next to his body. The killer left the knife this time, and it doesn't match Scott's wound."

"Poor Art." Sam's voice wavered. "He was special. I wish he would have confided in us more." Her stomach hurt, and she felt she might be sick.

"We'll find his killer. Roger and Jorge are tracking him now. I don't understand about these footprints, though." He pointed to the small deep prints. "I don't see them anywhere else, and why are they so deep? I want to talk to Tom, and he can try interviewing everyone again. It didn't go very well yesterday."

He's like a machine, processing the evidence. What about Art? What about the person? Her stomach heaved with her grief. She walked to the eastern side of camp, away from all the activity, and was violently ill.

Chapter 13

Roger and Jorge followed the two sets of footprints away from camp toward the west. Red ran back and forth, sniffing either side of the path and muddying up the prints. The tracks got increasingly less visible the farther they went until they couldn't see them anymore.

"The wind has been at our backs, Roger. Returning will be harder, no?"

"We should head back, huh."

"The tracks have disappeared."

The bite of the chill wind pummeled their chests and faces as they turned. "I'm glad we didn't go any farther. That would have been a mistake," Roger said, then was silent. The effort involved in pushing against the wind made him sweat, and the frigid air froze his lungs. He looked around for Red, who was staring mournfully at him, shivering. He picked him up and held him close. "Come on, boy, I know it's miserable."

Finally arriving back at camp, Roger set Red down by the fire and peeled off his jacket. "Got anything hot, Ben?"

Melissa hurried over to him with a towel. "What have you been doing out there? You're soaked."

"He carried that dog of his back here, against the wind. I'm half dead. I don't know how he did it."

"I walked next door with Jack yesterday, and it almost blew me over," Tom said. "It's really gusting."

Roger sat down and accepted a hot cup of coffee. "Where is Jack?"

Tom looked around. "I'm not sure. I haven't seen him for a while."

"We tried to follow the tracks into the woods but finally lost them. It was a lot easier on the way out than it was coming back."

"He'll probably finish soon, so have a rest and dry off."

"Would anyone like breakfast? No one has eaten yet."

"Thanks, Ben. I might be starving. Totally forgot about breakfast for a minute."

Jorge looked at Roger. "I sure didn't forget. I'm ready to eat several breakfasts."

Tom looked around the tent. Lisa and Hailey sat on their cots. Sissy was resting after having a dose of Melissa's calming tea. "Why don't you come have some breakfast, ladies?"

"What's going on outside?" Hailey asked. "No one told us anything."

"Sam's survival instructor was killed sometime last night. Sissy found him on the way to the restroom," Tom told her.

Lisa's eyes widened. "Why is all this happening? Who's doing this?"

"That's what we need to find out. We'll get everyone together and talk about it once Jack and Sam get back."

"What if they're dead too?" Hailey whispered. "Is someone out to get us all?"

Roger looked at the two women. "That's not very likely. Most murderers have a motive."

"Roger," Tom said. "Could you get me a cup of coffee?"

"Sure." He rose, knowing Tom was warning him not to say too much. He took him the coffee and mumbled an apology.

Tom smiled. "Thanks."

"Oh, breakfast! And coffee, I hope." Sam entered the tent with Jack, removed her jacket and went to kiss Tom on the cheek.

"You can have mine. It looks like an emergency."

"It sure is cold out there." She took a sip from the proffered cup and shivered.

"Roger walked back against the wind, carrying Red," Melissa said.

"My goodness, Roger. That sounds like quite a feat."

"Gotta take care of my pup, Ms. Sam."

Ben took plates to Jack and Sam.

"You don't have to wait on us, Ben."

"I know, but you just came in from the cold, and it's ready. I decided on pancakes today since I didn't know who was eating and when. This way, I can just cook a few whenever someone's ready." He chuckled.

"You have been such a god send. I don't know what we would have done without you."

"Starve, probably." He laughed. "I'm glad to help, Sam. Any idea what we're doing this afternoon? The storm is sure socked in."

"I'm not sure. We've gone through most of our indoor lessons and most of our food. It's horrible outside. Any ideas?"

"I could teach everyone how to whittle if you're interested. We could learn how to make fishhooks, spoons and forks, or cups from wood, with just a survival knife."

"That's a great idea, Roger. What do you think?" she asked the others.

Lisa shrugged.

"Sure," Hailey said.

Sissy moaned from over on her cot.

Jorge nodded.

"Okay, after breakfast, get your knives from your packs, and we'll make some cool souvenirs."

Sam cleared Tom's plate and her own after breakfast because he seemed deep in thought. In truth, he was carefully observing the campers to see where they got their knives from. One of them should be missing a knife. Lisa went straight to her pack and pulled hers out, bringing it to the table before removing the sheath. Hailey also went to a pack and rummaged around for hers, but he suspected it was Sissy's pack. Finally locating it, she also brought it to the table. Jorge had his attached to his belt. *I wonder where David is.*

All of them paid attention as Roger gave instructions, and he walked around the table to assist where needed. Once he had them all on the final, most time-consuming project, the bowl, he excused himself and went outside. He wandered around the campsite and crouched with a knife in his hand when he heard a branch crack in the woods behind the outhouse.

"It's just me," David whispered from a neighboring bush.

"Where have you been?" Roger whispered back. Hand on his rapidly beating heart.

"I witnessed what happened last night. I know where they pass messages, and I know where he's hiding. If they find out, they'll kill me too."

"Have you lost your mind?"

"Maybe. Remember how you told me I should be an investigative reporter?"

"Augh. I should learn to keep my mouth shut. Do you have a plan?"

"Yes, but I need to share information in case something happens to me."

"You should sleep indoors, at least. Do you expect them to drop a note tonight?"

"Maybe. I don't mind if someone else watches the drop location, though. I am frozen right through."

"Tell me what happened before we head in."

David looked around. "She led Art between the tents, then jumped on him, facing him, so her arms were around his neck and her legs were wrapped around him. She whispered something in his ear and kissed him. Then, she wrapped two hands around a big knife and drove it between his shoulder blades. When he started to fall, she leaped free, landing hard next to where he fell." David was breathing hard. "A man approached her and handed her a new jacket and gloves. After she changed, he took the bloody ones, then turned and walked into the woods. I followed him at a distance and hid when he got to a treehouse with a long ladder.

He climbed up to the platform, entered, lit a dim lamp inside, then he stayed there until dawn."

"Who was the woman?"

"Hailey."

Roger thought about that. "I did see a small footprint near where I found Scott."

"When she has a message for the man, she leaves it in a concealed wooden box attached to a tree near here. We need to wait for her to leave another message, then intercept it. I don't know who he is, but we need to catch him too."

"Did she see you?"

"I don't think so. I waited until she went inside before I followed the guy."

"Okay. Show me the location of the box, then let's get you warmed up in the second tent, and I'll try to get you some food. She can't leave during the day without someone noticing."

"Thanks. I'll admit I'm terrified. What she did? That was intense." David led him to the drop location and showed him where he hid before.

Roger nodded. "Follow me back and stay where you can see me, but don't cross until I tell you to." He walked along the eastern side of the second tent, where Scott and Art lay, then checked the passage in front of the tents. He waved for David to proceed, then accompanied him into the tent. "Get warmed up. I'll get Jack and some food."

He stood in front of the stove, teeth chattering. "Thanks again. I'm frozen to my bones."

Jack felt a tap on his back as Roger walked by. He excused himself and went to the stove, where he asked Ben for a cup of coffee. "We have a visitor in the second tent. Can you head over there without calling too much attention to yourself?"

"Sure. They are all caught up in fashioning the perfect bowl. Women are so competitive." He chuckled.

"Can I take him a plate, Ben?"

"David?"

"Yeah. Please don't mention it to anyone. He's in danger."

"This is sure a mysterious camp."

Roger sighed. "Very true."

He took the plate to David and waited with him while he ate. When Jack arrived, David repeated his story.

"So, we'll take shifts waiting for Hailey to make her move? Do we know the whereabouts of the tree, so we won't miss her?"

"Yeah. I'll show you," Roger said. "Get some sleep, David. I'll wake you up when it's your shift."

He went outside with Jack and showed him the drop location, then swept their foot-prints as they backed into the forest.

"How do we know he's telling the truth," Jack asked.

Roger put his finger to his lips, and they both stilled.

A gaunt man of medium height with long, greasy hair walked up to the drop box and put something inside, then, looking around furtively, disappeared back into the woods.

Jack and Roger remained still for several minutes after he left. "I guess that's how," Roger whispered. He crept forward and retrieved the note.

He opened it so Jack could see.

Followed. Unsafe. Blind. ASAP.

He replaced the note and retreated into the bushes. "We need a plan."

"The wind masks sound, but this guy is a pro. We need to stake out the blind on three sides and have a fourth person follow Hailey. That way, we can catch them together. I don't think he'll come down if she doesn't show."

"If she goes up, we won't be able to get at either of them." Jack pointed out.

"Someone at the bottom could nab her after she waves."

"Too late. Here she comes. How did she sneak away?"

"The loo."

Hailey approached the drop box and looked around. She took the note out, glanced at it, and started down the trail to the woods.

"Shoot. Are we even armed?" Roger asked.

"I have a gun in my pocket. Run back and get Jorge and a couple of rifles, then catch up."

"Okay. Don't do anything crazy."

Jack nodded.

Roger waited a few seconds, then ran back to camp. "Jorge, grab a rifle." He grabbed his and ran.

Sam looked at Tom, then put her jacket on and took another rifle. "Be right back." She smiled on her way out the door.

Once she cleared camp, she took off at a run. She spotted the tracks ahead and knew where they were headed.

Ducking behind a tree where he could see the blind, Jack saw Hailey wave, just as they had imagined, then head toward the ladder. With no backup, he surveyed the situation and waited. Roger and Jorge were about a minute behind him, then Sam showed up. "They're up there." He pointed. "Any ideas?"

"Let's spread out," Sam said. "When they come down, together or separately, we'll nab them. I brought duct tape."

Everyone snickered quietly.

Sam held the position, and the other three spread out. They got as close as they could while maintaining their cover and hunkered down to wait.

They heard arguing from above.

Finally, the door slammed, and Hailey climbed quickly down the ladder. When she reached the bottom, Jorge slapped a piece of duct tape across her mouth and drew her into the woods. She fought hard, but he kept hold of her.

"Holly!" The man in the blind called out softly. "Holly! Please be reasonable. He started down the stairs and Roger grabbed him when he had two feet to go. He applied another piece of duct tape and took the man's gun. "Let's go, folks. We've got them both."

The four reconvened and were ready to lead their captives back to the camp when Holly suddenly twisted and evaded Jorge's grasp. She raced into the woods with Sam right behind her. Dodging behind a tree, she stuck her foot out, and Sam tripped. The last thing Sam saw was Holly holding a large rock.

Jorge, Roger, and Jack stood by the blind with the man. When Sam didn't return after five minutes, Roger said, "You two take this guy to the second tent and watch for a possible ambush. I'll find Sam." He pulled out his flashlight and walked in the direction Sam had taken. I wish Red was with me. He didn't have to search for long. Sam was sit-ting up on the snowy path and gingerly feeling her head.

"What happened?"

"She tripped me, then hit me on the head. I think I'm bleeding. She took my knife, too."

"Any idea where she went?"

Sam started to shake her head, then stopped and groaned.

"Well, let's get back. I sent Jack and Jorge ahead with her brother."

Roger shone the flashlight on Sam's head. "You're bleeding, huh. Jack can examine that."

They walked back to camp and were greeted by a solemn-looking Melissa. "Hailey has Tom at knifepoint in the first tent. She is demanding we send you in there when you get back, but Tom did his little head shake when she said that. He looked at me and said towline, but I don't know what that means. Everyone else is in the second tent."

"It's a de-escalation technique he told me about. He said sometimes words work better than action. Maybe he can distract her until we figure out how to rescue him. He hasn't completely healed, and she's strong."

Chapter 14

Waving a knife, and screaming that Sam had ruined her life, Holly paced. Tom, trained in negotiations and de-escalation techniques, sat quietly, with an open posture, and said nothing.

She stopped in front of him. "Why aren't you saying anything?"

"Could you pull up a chair so I can look at you? My stitches make it hard for me to twist around."

"Why do you need to look at me?"

He tilted his head a little to the right and raised his eyebrows slightly. "I like to be able to see the person I'm talking to. I understand you're very angry, and I'd like to hear more about that."

She moved a chair to face him and flopped down. "You want to know why I'm angry?"

"Yes." He nodded. "You're angry at Sam?"

Holly looked at him, blinked rapidly, and looked away before resuming her rant. She was slightly more coherent but still driven by emotion.

Tom tried to focus on phrases she repeated. "You thought Sam was going to ruin your business?"

She nodded, then she shook her head. "Not ruin it, just take away customers."

Tom nodded. "Do you have the same kind of customers?"

Holly stopped to think about that. "No, I guess not. Our customers are more advanced and don't expect pampering. We would have been sleeping in emergency shelters and trapping squirrels, not staying in a fancy hot tent with a chef."

"It sounds like you cater to real survivalists. You must be incredibly good at what you do."

Holly nodded. "I am. I'm the best. Even Art said so." She looked at him more closely. "You seem nice. Why did you marry her?"

Tom tilted his head again. "Why were you with Art?"

"He was big and strong, and he liked me for me." She frowned. "Other women liked him too, and I was always afraid he was cheating."

"Was he?"

"I don't know. Maybe not." She stared at nothing.

"Do you think he and Sam were cheating on us?"

"She loves you a lot. Why isn't she in here?" Holly looked around the tent.

"I thought she was upsetting you."

"She was. She's the reason I'm here."

"You want to hurt me to punish her."

"Yes. No. I don't want to hurt you."

"Do you want Sam to come in and listen to you?"

"Yes."

"May I have the knife?"

Holly looked down at the knife in her hands and pulled it toward her. She shook her head, looked at it again, and slowly extended the handle to Tom with shaking hands. "She'll listen to me?"

"I promise."

He got up gingerly from the cot.

"Can I see your stitches?"

He turned and lifted his shirt.

Holly traced the stitches with her finger. "How did you get stitched up?"

"Jack did them with a needle and thread."

"That must have been very painful." She looked down. "I'm sorry you got shot."

"I think the stitches hurt more than the arrow." He gave her a small smile and went to get Sam.

Jack and Jorge took the man into the second tent and tied him securely to a chair. All the other campers were sitting huddled in the back of the tent. Ben had provided them with a snack after Holly demanded everyone leave the first tent.

"Hello." Jack pulled the duct tape off the man's mouth before taking a seat across from him. You're Holly's brother?"

"No."

"What's your name?"

"Ernie. Why do you think I'm Holly's brother?"

"Art told us. He was out in the woods with two of our staff when you killed Scott Jacobs."

"I didn't kill that guy. I didn't even know him."

"Holly told us you killed him because he was going to report your illegal hunting trips."

"Holly escaped and didn't tell you nothing."

"That's where you're wrong. Sam caught her. She also said that our witness made a mistake, and it was you who killed Art. She pointed out that if it had been her, she would have gotten blood on her ski jacket."

Ernie sat very still for a moment. Jack could almost see the wheels working as he thought about that. When Ernie clenched his fists, his mouth formed a hard, thin line. Jack knew he'd made his decision.

"I knew better than to come in between those two. I had nothing to do with his murder. Holly lured him out back and acted all lovey-dovey, then she stabbed him. I knew she planned it because she told me to bring her an extra ski jacket and gloves."

"Where did you get those?"

"She had them stashed in one of my hunting blinds."

"And you took the bloody ones back to the blind?"

"Yeah."

Jack leaned forward. "Tell me about Scott." Ernie paused, calculating again.

"He followed me from the camp. He didn't know who I was. Holly followed him through the trees, so he wouldn't see her footprints. I knew someone was following me, but I didn't know who, so I waited behind some bushes and ambushed him."

"You didn't know him?"

"I did, but he didn't know me. He fought me, and I stabbed him in self-defense. I didn't mean to kill him."

"If you didn't mean to kill him, why did you twist the knife?"

Ernie's brow furrowed. "It's just habit. When you're hunting, it's best to make sure your prey doesn't suffer."

"So, Holly saw you kill Scott?"

"Yeah, and she was spitting mad. She was about to let me have it when that guy and his dog showed up."

"Then what?"

"We hid until he left, then swept our prints. I went along the creek, and Holly looped back to camp."

"Thank you, Ernie." He started to leave, then turned back. "By the way, which of you is the expert archer?"

"That's Holly. I'll choose a gun every time."

"Do you know where we can find her bow?"

"It's in the blind with her other stuff."

Jack nodded. "I'll be back in a few minutes." He left the tent to confer with Roger.

"How's it going in there?"

"They're just talking right now."

"Bring her over when you get the chance."

Roger nodded and remained where he was, waiting outside with Sam in the cold.

Opening the tent flap, Tom leaned outside, ran his hand along Sam's jaw, and whispered, "TOWLINE."

Sam walked past him and sat on the cot across from Holly.

"You've got blood in your hair," Holly said.

"Yes."

Tom brought a folding chair and sat next to Holly. "Tell her why you were so angry."

"I want to tell you how you've ruined my life.

"I would like to understand. I've only known you as Hailey Jacobs. I don't really know anything about you."

"Art and I were a team. He loved me and always supported me. He never said no."

"He did love you. Very much."

Holly clenched her fists and leaned forward. "You don't get to talk about Art. You are the reason he's dead."

"Can you tell me more about that? Why I'm the reason he's dead?"

"Because when I got home from vacation, all he could talk about was you. 'Sam's so skilled. Sam's the best student I've ever had. I'm helping Sam set up her own business.' Whoa, I said. Sam's a woman? And you're setting her up to compete with us?" Holly's brow furrowed, and her mouth pursed. "He didn't see a problem with that. Not only didn't he recognize when a woman was hitting on him, he was generous to a fault. Next thing I knew, he'd be partners with someone else."

Sam nodded and leaned forward. "You thought I was trying to steal Art and your business."

"Yes. You can see how it looked."

"I can. Yes. Why didn't you tell me?"

"I told Art to tell you. I told him that you couldn't build your business here. He didn't do anything, so my brother said he'd help me stop you, but nothing worked. We tried simple sabotage, I tried scaring you with an arrow, and we even drove you away from camp. You were like the roadrunner. You have some kind of devilish luck."

"You were trying to get rid of me or the camp whatever way you could."

"Yes! But then you disappeared, and your camp was still there."

"That must have been frustrating."

"It was. And then my jerk brother killed Scott. He was my best friend. He always looked out for me. I was so angry."

Sam nodded. "That would make me angry too."

"If only Art could have minded his own business. He kept chasing Ernie around and interfering. He told me he couldn't condone murder."

Sam tipped her head slightly to the side.

"Ernie started telling me that Art was going to kill both of us if we didn't do something. He put thoughts in my head."

"So, Ernie made you think you had to kill Art?"

"I told you it's your fault Art died." Holly got up and started to pace again. "If you hadn't dazzled him, and if you hadn't started this camp, none of this would have happened." She went stomping toward the door and right into Roger's arms.

"Hello, there. I was just looking for you."

"Me?"

"Yes, perhaps you would like to join us in the second tent."

"Sometimes, I underestimate your skills." Sam lunged forward and hugged Tom.

"I know." He grinned at her. "You remembered TOWLINE. I wasn't sure you were really listening to me when I was explaining it."

"I'm a great mult-itasker. I'm not sure I remember all of it, but I understood what we were doing."

"Good enough. You did an excellent job."

"That's just because you already had her de-escalated before I came in. Should we go see what's going on in the other tent?"

"It might be better if she doesn't associate us with her interrogation. We were sitting here talking to her when she stormed out. Let's let Jack take over now."

Roger and Jorge secured Hailey to the empty chair next to Ernie. Ernie wouldn't look at her.

Jack observed the two suspects. "We have a witness that saw you, Hailey, or Holly, kill Art in cold blood. He claims that you ran and hugged him, with your arms and legs around him, then lifted a knife with both hands and stabbed him between his shoulder blades."

Holly recovered quickly. "Do you see my size? How on earth would I stab such a large man?"

"How do you know he's a large man?"

"You just said I wrapped my legs around him."

"Couldn't you wrap your legs around a smaller man?"

She stared at him.

"Also, Art told us about your relationship and about how you threatened him."

"Why would he let me get so close to him if he didn't trust me? Maybe your so-called witness is lying. Who was it? Lisa maybe? The one who is always leaving camp for some mysterious reason?"

"She does have a point," Sissy interjected.

Lisa stood and clenched her fists.

"Would the three of you please go get some coffee in the first tent?" Roger said.

Lisa, Sissy, and David filed out of the tent. David looked back as he left.

Jack turned back to Holly. "Let's return to our questioning."

"I think we're done," Hailey spat.

"Not quite. There is the matter of Scott's murder. We know there was no ex-husband, you were not in the tent when Roger returned, and he found a single, small footprint by the creek. A footprint that matches yours. Did you kill Scott after he tried to help you?"

"Of course not. Scott was my best friend."

"If you didn't, then Ernie did, and you were there."

She struggled against the cordage binding her to the chair. "How did you come up with that brilliant piece of logic?"

Art told us about your brother. He's an ex-con who runs illegal hunting trips in the mountains and would do anything for you.

Roger and Jorge chased Ernie through the woods while he was dragging Scott's body, but they also discovered your footprint near the creek."

"Fine. Ernie killed him. Scott was talking about reporting Ernie's activities to the Feds. I was so mad, but it was done. Ernie made me help clear his tracks and sent me back to camp. He said he'd take care of it."

"And Art?"

"I loved Art. I would never hurt him."

"So that was Ernie, too?"

"Ernie would never try to come between us."

"Ernie told us you killed Art."

"What?" She turned and stared at Ernie. "You told them what?"

"It's your fault for telling them I did it."

"Unlike you, I would never throw you under the bus."

"Like you just did when they asked you about Scott? And when you told them that it had to be me because you didn't have blood on your jacket? After you told me to take you an extra one?"

"It's my word against his," Holly said smugly.

"Unless your bloody jacket is in the blind where Ernie said it was."

"Are you kidding me?" She looked at him with wide eyes, and he shrugged.

When the three campers entered the first tent, Lisa wheeled around and glared at Sissy. "You have a lot of nerve."

Sissy and David were looking at Sam, who was on her knees with her head on Tom's lap. "What happened," David asked.

"Holly had a knife pointed at Tom, and he talked her down."

"Holly? You mean Hailey?" Sissy asked.

"Her real name is Holly. What are you guys arguing about?"

"Hailey, or Holly, accused me of being the witness, and Sissy had to chime in. I'm not the witness, but I guess I should explain." She looked directly at Sam.

"My fiancé came out here on a hunting trip several months ago and never came home. The police looked for him and even got the park rangers involved, but they didn't find any sign of him. I hired a private investigator, but he finally gave up too. I wanted to keep looking, but I knew I couldn't survive out here on my own, so I signed up for your camp. I've been out searching every day."

"Why didn't you tell us? We could have helped you."

"I thought you might be angry, and you've certainly had enough on your plates." She looked down.

"He came up here with a group?" Tom asked.

"Yes, I don't remember the name of the group, but the leader's name was Ernie."

Sam gasped. "Ernie? The guy in the other tent?"

"I don't know if it's the same guy, but how many Ernies can be running hunting trips in this forest?"

"We'll need to question him again." Tom frowned.

Ben entered the tent and asked if anyone would like some lunch. "I can make something simple. Sandwiches?"

"That will be great, Ben." Sam stood and put her hand on Tom's shoulder. "Do we have any more coffee?"

"Yeah." Ben poured her a cup. "And the storm broke. A few slivers of sunlight are shining through the clouds."

"Thank goodness." She took a sip of coffee and sighed happily.

Tom got up from the chair and moved to his cot. "How's it going next door?"

"Fairly well. Ernie was making noise about having to use the restroom when I left."

"Do you want to see if they need a hand, David? I'm trying to keep myself and Sam out of it since we were trying to play good cop in here."

David nodded and left the tent.

Jack and Roger untied Ernie and escorted him to the portable outhouse. It consisted of a five-gallon bucket with a seat and a bag, covered by a zip-up privacy tent staked to the ground on four corners. They waited outside the entrance. After a minute, they heard a loud ripping sound. "He wouldn't," Roger said, looking around the side of the outhouse. "He did." Roger took off at a run, Jack on his heels."

Suddenly Roger stopped. "Forget it, Jack. He's headed back toward town. As soon as the snowcats come, we'll report him."

Jack stood next to him, panting. "For someone so dumb, he has a lot of creativity."

"There are various kinds of smart and dumb. He's... wily, no?"

"Yes. That's a good word for him. I'm not looking forward to telling Tom he escaped."

Holly smirked when they entered the tent. "He got away, huh."

"The sheriff will pick him up easily enough," Roger said. "I'll go get some sandwiches and let the others know. Our meal schedule has been off today. I'm starving."

"Hey, I'm hungry too."

"I can feed you if you like, but we're not losing another one. The sheriff should be here soon. Come on, David." He could see Holly working at the cordage, but he was proud of his work and certain she wouldn't be getting free any time soon.

"After lunch, let's start to pack up some of our stuff. The snowcats should be here soon." Sam looked around. "We have a lot of gear scattered around."

Sissy sat down next to Jack, who immediately recoiled. "Jack, why are you always avoiding me? I came to this camp thinking maybe we could get to know each other better."

"You act like a stalker. I don't even know you. Are you really a schoolteacher?"

"Of course." She grinned. "I met you when you came to our school and gave a presentation for career day. You were so nice, and all the kids loved you. I thought we kind of had a connection."

"I only did a career day once, and the only person I met was..."

Sissy smiled. "It was me."

"But you look completely different."

"I was in a terrible car accident. I was in the hospital for a long time and lost a lot of weight, then I had to have reconstructive surgery on my face. Is that why you've been avoiding me? You didn't recognize me?"

He pulled his wallet out of his back pocket and opened it up, sliding a newspaper article out of the middle. He carefully unfolded it and handed it to her. The caption beneath the black and white photo read Chief Medical Examiner, Jack Olivares, with Ms. Wong at Sunnyside Elementary career day. They were smiling, but Ms. Wong looked like someone else.

"I have that picture too."

"That was two years ago. I wish you would have let me know."

Sissy smiled sadly. "I had no idea you wouldn't recognize me at all."

Sam got up and walked around the table. "May I see?" She held out her hand. Sissy handed her the picture, and Sam studied it. The woman in the picture had a smiling, round face and short, curly hair. *She reminds me of Ally.* Sam glanced at Jack. "You do look quite different. I probably wouldn't have recognized you either. That looks like a happy memory." She handed the picture back.

Jack looked at the picture again and put it back in his wallet, then he turned to Sissy and said, "Nice to meet you again, Ms. Wong. It's been a long time."

Chapter 15

Everyone stopped and listened to the approaching engine. "The snowcats!" Sam jumped up and ran outside. A lone snowmobile pulled up near the tents and she tilted her head, perplexed, when Anita climbed out of the cab. "Are you alone?"

"Just for now. There was an accident."

"An accident? Was anyone seriously injured?"

"I'm afraid so. A man came running down the mountain and right in front of the first snowcat. Carlos couldn't stop in time. Mick recognized the victim and called for an ambulance and backup."

"Was it Ernie?"

Anita looked at Sam in surprise. "Yes, Ernie Cooper. He's wanted for violating his parole. Carlos is pretty shaken up."

"We've had a lot going on up here. Ernie escaped, but his sister, Holly, is still in our custody."

Anita shook her head. "I didn't know Ernie had a sister. At least you keep us busy."

"Hey!"

Anita chuckled. "Mick should be up here soon, I hope."

Sam invited her inside the tent and got her some hot coffee. "This is Deputy Flores, for those of you who don't know her. Ernie got hit by one of the snowcats on his way down the mountain, so the others have been delayed."

"Is he okay?" Sissy asked.

"Okay is not a word I would use, but he might live."

Lisa's brow furrowed, and she mumbled something.

Anita sat down and sipped her coffee.

Mick and Carlos finally pulled into camp and joined the others in the tent. "Sorry, we're so late." Mick stopped and looked around. "What's going on here?"

"You might want to take Holly Cooper into custody before anything else happens; then we can recap," Tom suggested.

"What are we charging her with?"

"Murder and attempted murder. Ernie also, but I hear he's been detained."

"Is she in the other tent?"

"Yes, and she's dangerous, so don't let your guard down."

Mick stepped into the second tent, followed by Carlos. Holly was bound to a folding chair, and Jack, Roger, and Jorge were sitting on cots discussing livestock. "Hello everyone; we're here to take Ms. Holly Cooper into custody. Carlos, could you read her her rights, please?"

"You have the right to remain silent. Anything you say can and will be used against you in a court of law. You have the right to an attorney. If you cannot afford an attorney, one will be provided for you. Do you understand the rights I have just read to you?"

"Yes."

"Okay. Let's take a trip to the station." He released her from the chair, and before he could place the handcuffs on her wrists, she kicked him and twisted around, running for the door.

"That's enough, Holly." Mick took her forearm in his large paw and stopped her. "Are you alright, Carlos?"

"Yes, sir. Sorry, sir." Carlos limped over and put the cuffs on Holly's wrists.

"Why don't you take Anita with you? Call for backup when you get down to the road."

Holly smirked.

Mick accompanied them to the snowcat and made sure Holly was secure, then followed Jack into the first tent.

"Why don't we go in the second tent and have a debrief?" Jack suggested.

"Are you coming, Tom?"

"I think I need to rest. Jack can fill you in, and we'll talk later."

"Rest?" Mick said as they left the tent.

"Yeah. Roger should come too because we were separated for a while." He jogged back and asked Roger to join them, then entered the second tent and found David sitting on his cot whittling. He looked up at Roger. "Who's that?"

"This is Sergeant Mickelson from the Santo Milagro sheriff's office. Mick, this is David Arndt, one of our campers."

"Should he be part of this conversation?"

"Yes, I think so."

Sam entered the tent. "I'd like to be part of this too."

Mick nodded. "Let's start at the beginning."

"First, there was the sabotage," Roger said. "It was irritating and potentially hazardous, but no one got hurt. We forgot to ask Holly and Ernie about that."

Mick wanted details, so they filled him in, and he took notes. "What happened after that?"

"A shooter with a bow and arrow took a shot at Sam, then hit Tom in the back," Roger said.

"I'm surprised he's up and about."

"The arrow hit something in his pack and bent slightly. He was incredibly lucky. Sam got a graze in her arm, also lucky."

"Do we know who the shooter was?"

"Yes, it was Holly. Ernie told us where to look for her weapons. We can go there after our debrief."

Mick was nodding and writing.

"Sam let off a flare and covered us while we got Tom back to camp, then headed further up the mountain."

"I never did figure out why Ernie and I didn't run into each other up there. Someone was staying in a hunting blind because fresh footprints looped around the area."

Sam got a faraway look in her eye as she thought back.

"I wonder if Lisa's fiancé might be hiding out up there," Jack said. "We should check it out later."

"What about a fiancé?" Mick looked up.

"It's a separate story," Sam said. "Let's stick to this one for now. Jack met up with me at a cave we've been to before, and Art followed him."

"Art? Jimenez? How do you know him?"

"He was my survival instructor. He's dead now."

Mick sighed. "What happened to him?"

"Not yet. He told us that his business partner, also his girlfriend, Holly, wanted me out of the way because she thought Art had a romantic interest in me and thought my business would interfere with theirs and her brother's. She threatened him and told him not to interfere. We knew her as Hailey, and she signed up for camp with her husband, Scott Jacobs."

"She was married?"

"No, but she said she was."

"What kind of business did her brother have?"

"He was running illegal hunting camps up here."

"I'm not surprised."

"Anyway, the storm was rolling in, and I convinced Jack that we needed to get back to camp. We had almost made it here when the wind kicked up, and someone shot at us. We thought it was probably Ernie." Sam looked at Jack. "We forgot to ask him about that too."

"Sam returned fire, and he went down, so we continued here and asked Roger and Art to go back with us to check on him. When we got back, he was gone."

"The hospital will be able to tell us if he has any recent gunshot wounds."

"Oh. We got back after Scott was killed. Roger can tell you about that," Sam said.

"Sounds like it was Armageddon up here." Mick's eyebrows were up near his hairline.

"We found out what happened after the fact," Roger began, "but what Ernie told us was Scott followed him from camp, and Holly followed Scott. Ernie knew someone was following him, so he ambushed him. Scott didn't know who Ernie was, so he fought back, and Ernie stabbed him. They heard us coming, so Ernie dropped Scott in the creek, and he and Holly hid."

"Who's us?"

"Me and Red. I came upon Scott and assumed he was dead, and I noticed Ernie's footprints. I wasn't sure what to do, so I returned to camp for help."

"Are you sure it was self-defense?"

"No. That's what Ernie told us. I went back with Melissa and Jorge, but the body was gone."

"Sounds like a recurring theme." Mick was still taking notes. "Who's Jorge? Sanchez?"

"Yeah. He's one of the campers.

"He's been having a tough time. I'm glad he was able to join the camp." He noticed Sam's quizzical look. "I'll tell you about it later. Go ahead, Roger."

"We looked in both directions and finally found the spot where Ernie left the creek. He had Scott on his back and was dragging his feet. I set Red on his trail, and he found Scott in some bushes."

"Was he alive?"

"Just barely. We left Melissa and Red with him and continued following the tracks. We didn't catch him. He shot at us from a blind in the trees, then escaped when we were interrupted by Art, who was also following him."

"So, Ernie got away."

"Yes. Art followed him and told us to head back, that he'd come later to talk to Tom. Melissa did her best, and we carried Scott back to camp, but he died in transit."

"How did Holly react to Scott's death?"

"She acted distraught, but we found out later she was there when Ernie stabbed him.

We also found one of her footprints in the snow. They missed one."

Mick looked at his notes. "Sam and Jack returned after Scott died and after Art showed up."

"Yes. When the storm started to blow, he asked if he could have food and a cot, but he didn't want the female campers to know he was here."

"I guess we know why."

"This is where David comes in. He's fearless and wants to be an investigative reporter. Did I mention crazy? I'll let you take over, David."

"Can I have the exclusive on this?" he winked at Roger. "Art snored really loud, so when his snoring stopped, it woke me up. I saw him talking to someone through the tent door and putting on his jacket, so I decided to follow him."

"I woke up too," Roger said. "A draft from outside and the sudden quiet. Do you know what time it was?"

"I'm not sure. I went around the side of the tent, where the bodies are, and looked around back.

"Wait. Where the bodies are?"

"There was only one at the time, Scott's. Anyway, Hailey ran and jumped on Art, but he didn't seem to mind. Her arms and legs were wrapped around him, and their faces were close. I think he was talking in her ear and kissing her, then she held a knife up behind him and grabbed it with both hands and hit him hard like she put all her strength behind it. When he fell, she jumped to the side, so he didn't land on her."

"What was he doing with his hands? He let go of her?"

"His knees buckled, and he put his hands out to catch himself. It could have gone badly for her if he hadn't."

"So, she jumped free. Did she have blood on her clothes?"

"Yeah. A lot. There was so much blood. The guy you were interviewing stepped out from behind the outhouse. She took off her jacket and gloves and traded him for clean ones. They talked for a minute, then she went back inside. I followed him into the woods to his tree house."

"Tree house?"

"His hunting blind," Roger clarified. "That was Ernie."

David nodded. "I found out who he was when you brought him in."

"How did you find out about their drop box?"

"I was watching Hailey because she was behaving strangely. She put a note in there, so I pulled it out and read it. Then I waited to see who came for the note."

"That was before the murder?" Mick asked.

"Yes."

"What did the note say?"

"Tonight."

"That's it?"

David nodded.

"After David nearly gave me a heart attack, sneaking up on me outside, I got him warmed up in the second tent, and we decided to take turns watching the drop. When Ernie left a message for Hailey to meet him at the blind, we waited for her to retrieve the message and followed her," Roger said. "That's how we captured them."

Mick was writing again. "Who's we?"

"Me, Jack, Jorge, and Sam. Unfortunately, Holly got away, like she almost did with Carlos. Sam went after her and ended up with a bloody head. Holly came here and held Tom at knifepoint while they waited for Sam."

Mick was speechless.

"Tom talked Holly down, then invited Sam in for some more discussion. Holly got mad about something and stomped out of the tent right into my waiting arms."

Mick shook his head and leaned forward, waiting for whatever came next.

"Jack had already interviewed Ernie and tricked him into telling him what happened, so when I took Holly in, he got the rest of the story. Then Ernie told us he had to go to the bathroom and outsmarted us by slicing through the outhouse tent and running down the mountain."

"He came barreling down the mountain and ran right into the path of a snowcat," Mick said. "If he makes it, he'll be going back to prison for a very long time." He stood. "Let's go check out the blind."

Mick, Roger, Jack, and Sam went to the blind, where they found the bow and arrows and the bloody jacket and gloves. By the time the evidence had been secured, Anita and Carlos were back. They moved the bodies onto one of the snowcats.

Jack said, "Could you have the evidence and the bodies taken to the morgue in Las Rodillas? I'll examine them myself when I get back."

Ben served lunch, and Sam told Mick about Lisa's missing fiancé. "There's a possibility that Ernie was the organizer of that hunting trip."

"I was hoping we could ask him about it," Lisa said. "Now he's in the hospital and could die with that knowledge."

"I saw footprints near where Jack and I stayed on the mountain. I thought they were Ernie's, but now I'm not so sure. I think we should check it out."

"It will be much quicker in a snowcat. Everyone ready to go?"

"I'll sit this one out since you've already got four," Jack said. "Maybe Tom will share his jerky."

"You heard about that? Lisa won it all last game. How about another sandwich?"

The others loaded into the snowcat, and Sam gave Mick directions. When they got to the blind, Mick could see why Sam thought someone was around. "What's his name, Lisa?"

"Kevin." She was trembling, and Sam put her arm around her shoulders.

"Anyone there?" Mick called out. "This is Sergeant Mickelson of the Santo Milagro sheriff's office. "Kevin? Are you there?"

"Cover me," he told the others and proceeded to climb the ladder to the blind.

He was inside for a minute, then backed down the ladder. "Someone's been living here, but they aren't here now. Are there any fresh prints down there?"

"This way." Roger led the party away from the blind, angling toward the cave where Sam and Jack stayed. "They aren't Ernie's tracks. They're too fresh."

They got back inside the snowcat and followed the tracks toward the waterfall. Mick parked by the frozen pool of water.

"Let's spread out. Sam, you come with me. I'm not sure where to look."

She led him along the narrow trail behind the waterfall and noted that her makeshift gate had been moved. She motioned to Mick to follow her as she walked quietly to the second cove. A tall, emaciated man in ragged clothing lolled in a fetal position near the food locker. "Kevin?" she said quietly.

He rolled over and groaned.

"Are you Kevin?"

He nodded.

"What happened?"

She couldn't hear his response, so she got on her knees and put her ear down by his mouth. Suddenly his hands flew up and grabbed her throat. She was choking and didn't know what to do, so she punched him in the face. Blood spurted from his nose, and he let go. "You'd better get Lisa and see if she can identify him," she told Mick.

"Lisa? You have Lisa?"

"She's been looking for you for months if you're Kevin." She handed him a small towel to help stanch the bleeding.

"Be careful," Sam said. "He might have lost a grip on his sanity. He tried to strangle me. I'd hate to have to shoot him."

Lisa looked at her with wide eyes and put her hand to her throat, then looked at the man on the ground. "Kevin?"

"Lisa," he groaned and held out his hand. "Is that really you? They told me they'd kill you if I told anyone."

"Told anyone what?"

"It's a long story. Right now, I think I might die."

"Why? What's wrong?"

"Let me take a guess. Kevin is near starvation. He has gone hungry for long periods of time. Then he found my stash of food and gorged himself. His tiny, starving stomach is probably in excruciating pain. Is that right?"

"Probably." He groaned again. "And I think you broke my nose."

He sounds like it. "If we can get him to the snowcat, he'll be much more comfortable in the hot tent. What do you say, Kevin?"

"Warm sounds good."

"How are you even alive? Do you have a jacket?" Mick asked.

"I found that." He pointed to a reflective bag with holes cut for his arms and feet. "I think it saved my life."

Roger entered the cave and helped Mick get Kevin to the snowcat. Lisa sat next to him, and he held onto her like she might vanish. Sam kept a wary eye on him and maintained her distance.

Everyone gathered around the table in the first tent. Roger and Ben handed out coffee. Melissa made a special tea for Kevin and some for herself while Jack checked Kevin's vital signs to make sure he wasn't in any immediate danger. "My advice is to get checked into the hospital so they can make sure you're okay."

"Can I stay here one night, where I can be with Lisa? I don't want to go to the hospital tonight."

"Does anyone want to go back tonight?" Sam asked.

Tom put his hand in the air, but she gave him a slight shake of her head, so he put it back down.

"I think I'm ready to go," David said.

"Me too. But I hope you'll call me when you get back to Burque," Sissy told Jack.

"I guess I'm ready." Jorge raised his hand.

"I'm ready too," Ben said, "but I don't want you guys to starve."

"We'll be okay for one night." Sam smiled.

"I'd like to get back and see to the animals, but I don't want to leave you guys to break camp by yourselves, so I'll stay."

"Thanks, Roger." Sam smiled. "Could you take these four back with you, Mick, and come back up in the morning? We'll have breakfast and break down the camp."

"About ten?"

"Sounds good. Thank you."

Chapter 16

That evening, they sat around the table and ate leftovers. Kevin ate slowly and made sure he didn't overindulge like he had the last time. Lisa encouraged him to drink plenty of water. By the time they had finished dinner, he was able to tell them some of his story.

"I joined a hunting group that came up here in the fall. Everyone seemed to know it was illegal except for me. Someone bagged a giant buck, and we were all celebrating around the campfire. When I went to relieve myself, I stepped into a hole and sprained my ankle. The next day, a ranger was poking around. The other men hid the deer and left me in the blind because I couldn't walk quickly. The leader told me if I ratted them out, he would kill Lisa, then come back for me."

Lisa leaned against him and rubbed his arm.

"That's rough. Was Ernie the organizer?" Roger said.

"No, but he's the one who stayed with us. The owner's name was…." He shook his head. "I don't remember."

"You were left alone in the hunting blind?" Tom prompted.

"Yeah. I didn't know what to do. I didn't even know where I was. The ranger left; maybe he followed them, I don't know. No one ever came back. I cut up the deer and packed some of it in salt, dried some of it, cooked and ate some of it. There were some cans of food in the blind, and as my ankle got better, I gathered some nuts. The weather was getting colder, and I started running low on food and water."

Everyone was riveted by his story. No one made a sound, yet he stopped. "Could I have some more tea?"

"Of course." Melissa got up and brewed him some.

"You might wonder why I stayed at the blind, and the answer to that is, I don't know. At first, I couldn't walk. Then I started getting cold and hungry, but I didn't know how to get back to town. I was worried that I might run into that guy again or get lost and have no shelter. I don't think my mind was working very well."

Melissa brought him his tea.

"Does anyone want more coffee?" Sam asked.

Several hands went up, so she went over to the stove to make some.

"Do you want me to continue?" Kevin asked.

"Yes!" It was unanimous.

"I'm almost at the end. I was almost at my end, I think. I hadn't eaten for days, and I started seeing snowshoe prints around the blind. The day the storm hit, I saw you two, Sam and Jack? You were heading away from the waterfall with packs. If my brain had been functioning, I would have asked you if I could join you or at least followed you, but instead, I headed for the waterfall. I found the cave, the rocket stove, the wood, the food, and water. I was so excited I was almost giddy. I lit the stove and sat in front of it until I fell asleep. The next day I started to eat. I ate and ate until I was sick."

He looked at Sam. "When you came back, I thought you were going to take the food away. I'm sorry I choked you."

"That didn't even occur to me. I'm sorry too."

"I think people return to their primitive instincts when they start to starve and dehydrate. I was not even a person anymore. You were looking for me this whole time?"

Lisa's eyes were shiny when she nodded. "I was out in the storm every day, but I didn't go up high enough. Ernie got hit by a snowcat today, by the way. He's in the hospital."

Kevin shivered. "I'm glad I'm not there then."

"He can't hurt you now. They aren't sure he's going to make it."

"When he doesn't, you can check me in. It feels so good to be warm."

"Hey," Jack said, "what's a rocket stove?"

"It looked brand new."

"It was." Sam smiled. "I was trying things out for the survival camp. A rocket stove has a chute to insert wood. The wood burns inside, and you can cook on the top. It releases less light and smoke than a regular stove or campfire."

"Why didn't we use it?"

"It still releases some light and smoke. I was being careful. I remember how happy I was to be warm again, Kevin. I can't even imagine being out there all that time without even a snow suit."

"I don't know if I ever want to go out in the woods again, but if I do, I want a tent like this."

"I'd like you and Lisa to be my special guests if we do this again. You can stay warm and eat delicious, filling meals."

"It was a wonderful camp, Sam, except for the murders and the storm. I wouldn't mind trying it again."

"Murders?"

"I'll tell you later, honey. Another long story."

The next morning, everyone rose with the sun, and Jack set about making bacon and eggs while Sam and Roger broke down the second tent. Everyone had packed up their personal belongings the night before, and they let Kevin sleep in, figuring it was the first good night's sleep he'd had in a long time. They folded up the other cots, then sat down together for their final camp meal.

Sam looked around at all of them and smiled. "I'm sorry that this camp turned out to be so traumatic. I'm glad that you were all here with me, though. I felt safer knowing I had friends I could rely on."

"Are you going to have another camp?" Melissa asked.

"I'm not sure. I have to admit, staying in that cold cave with nothing but survival food to eat is not something I want to do again, and having a murderer skulking about and no way to call for help was terrifying and unsafe. Maybe if we did it again, we could have someone check in on us every day or two. I need to think about it."

They all stayed seated when Kevin got up, and Jack placed a big plate of breakfast and a cup of Melissa's tea in front of him. He grinned and ate every bite.

When he was done, they worked together to pack up all the cooking supplies, so everything was ready except the one stove. Sam didn't think that anyone should be cold while they waited, especially Kevin.

When Mick, Carlos, and Anita arrived, Sam put the stove outside and helped stow the gear in the snowcats. "How's Ernie doing, Mick?"

"He's still hanging on. We had to send Holly to Las Rodillas. She's a handful."

Sam shook her head. "Poor Art. He really loved her, even though he knew she had gone too far. I'll miss him." She pulled Mick aside. "What were you saying about Jorge?" she asked quietly.

Mick glanced around. "His wife left, and he's been isolating. I don't think he's been away from his ranch for months."

"Thank you for telling me. He was great in a crisis. We were glad to have him here."

"I think he'll be okay now." Mick nodded and put his hand on Sam's shoulder before approaching Anita, who was finished loading gear into her snowcat. Sam hugged Lisa and Keven and told them to stay in touch before they joined Anita for their ride down the mountain.

"We will," Lisa said, "I want you at our wedding."

It took a little longer to pack up the rest of the gear, but they were down the hill and transferring their things into Sam's truck before noon.

"Come on over," she told her friends, "I am craving pizza and Modelo. There is no denying it."

"That's my cuz," Jack said. "I'm in."

"Could Roger take me home so I can shower first? I feel gross." Melissa wrinkled her nose.

"Yes. Showers all around. That sounds wonderful."

"I seem to remember you talking about a hot bath." Tom winked.

"I wonder how long the hot water will last."

"Why don't you run your bath, and Tom and I will share whatever's left," Jack said. "You can go first, Tom, and I will order the pizza."

They pulled into the drive at Sam's ranch, and she hopped out of the truck and ran to the barn. Tom and Jack looked at each other and said, "Ghost." Then they both smiled.

"At least she's consistent," Jack said.

"I'll go up and run her bath, then I'll be back to unload the truck."

"I'll give you a hand. That way, when we're done, maybe the water will be hot again."

Tom turned and approached the house, letting himself in with his shiny new key. *I'm happy to be home. Home. Home with my adventurous bride.* He smiled.

Sam exited the barn and walked over to Jack with a smile. "She missed me."

"Of course she did."

"Where's Tom?"

"He went to run your bath. He said he'll be back to help unload. Go have a soak."

"Thanks. You don't have to tell me twice." She jogged to the side door.

Jack stood by the truck waiting. *Sam and I are just where we should be. I'm glad she found Tom. He nodded to himself and began unloading the truck.*

Sam stayed in the tub for a long time. The hot water soothed her sore muscles and warmed her in a way nothing else could do. By the time she got out, put on her pajamas, and wrapped herself in a long, fuzzy robe, everyone else was downstairs eating pizza.

Chiquito was winding around her feet, so she picked him up and scratched his head. "Hey. You didn't wait for me?"

"We weren't sure you were ever going to get out."

"The pizza was my idea."

"Don't worry. Jack ordered enough to feed an army," Tom said around a large bite.

"He ordered a large pizza for each of us." Melissa laughed.

"Awesome. Give me mine." Sam bounced a little and held out her hands.

Jack handed her a pizza. She took the box and opened it. She stared at it, then frowned. Tom handed her a Budweiser, and she frowned harder. She looked at them in confusion. Then everyone laughed. "Here," Jack said. "I'm just playing." He handed her another box and a Modelo Negra.

She opened the new box of pizza, and there, with steam still rising, was her favorite— pepperoni, pineapple, and jalapeno. She breathed in deeply. "It smells so good." Then she took a bite and almost swooned. The combination of sweet and tangy, salty, spicy, and savory perfection was almost more than she could bear. Her eyes closed. "Oh, I missed this so much. I was dreaming about it in that cold cave." She opened her eyes and looked at Jack. "I thought you had lost your mind. There were vegetables in that box." She shuddered.

"It was a great joke, though." He grinned.

"It was a pretty good one." Sam took another bite.

"Where's Preciosa?"

"She's curled up in my lap. I guess she remembered me," Jack said happily.

"If you take her, Chiquito will be heartbroken." Chiquito wound himself around the rungs of Jack's chair as if making sure Jack understood.

"I won't. I'm not home enough. She would be lonely."

"It looks like he remembers you too."

"I have to go to my new job tomorrow," Tom said out of the blue. "Not too much rest for the weary."

"I'll be going into Las Rodillas to see about the autopsies. Let's touch base in the afternoon and see how the case is progressing."

"Everyone has something important to do except me," Sam said.

"You have the important task of reviewing your first camp and deciding on which changes you'll make for the next one," Tom said.

"I'm not sure I want to do that again."

"Perhaps you'll decide not to, but you owe it to yourself to review everything and make an informed decision."

Sam sighed. "I might feel differently after I've had some more pizza."

Once Roger took Melissa home, Jack set the alarm, and he, Tom, and Sam headed upstairs.

Tom followed him to his room and asked, "Is there any particular reason you set the alarm?"

"Not really, but since there's been so much going on, I thought it a good precaution."

Tom nodded. "See you in the morning."

"You'll smell it. We have a ritual when I'm here. I have coffee and breakfast ready by the time Sam gets up."

Tom laughed and went down the hall to join Sam. She was already snuggled under the blankets in a ball. "I don't know if I'll ever feel warm again."

"You will. I promise." He climbed in and snuggled up to her, and they were asleep in seconds.

Alice Kanaka

Chapter 17

The next morning, Sam awoke to an empty house. Well, not exactly empty. Both cats came running when she opened her bedroom door. "You guys just want food. I bet you already ate." She walked into the kitchen, poured a cup of coffee, scooped up some eggs and bacon, then sat down at the table, where she found a note.

Dear hard-working, angelic wife (is that too thick?),
I am off to my first day of work. Cross your fingers that we don't have any high-profile missing cows. Our house-hubby, Jack, offered to make me lunch, but I suspect we may meet for lunch in Las Rodillas. Stay vigilant and keep the alarm on when you're in the house, just for now.
I love you more!
Tom

P.S. Jack here. Tom is obnoxious in the morning and should not be allowed to speak until after breakfast. XO

She looked down at Chiquito, who was rubbing against her ankles again. "You're sure friendly. Are you trying to tell me something?" She picked him up and stroked him while she drank her coffee. "Those two will probably end up best friends. I need to go out and see Antoine." She smiled at the thought of her heritage turkey's happy gobbling. *He's probably lonely too, but first, I think I'll have another hot bath.* She put Chiquito down and went upstairs to start the bath, then went back downstairs to finish her breakfast and pour herself another cup of coffee.

I don't know why I feel so cold and tired. She got in the bath and drank her coffee, then got out, dried, and got back into bed.

Tom reported for duty at seven, but no one else was at the station. He walked down the street to the Ugly Orange Café and was surprised to see it was open. The little bell on the door jingled as he walked in.

"Buenos días," the waitress called. "Café?"

"Yes, please."

"You're Mr. Sam, no? I was at the wedding."

Tom smiled. "Yes, I'm Tom. Thank you for coming."

"I'm Claudia. Anita, my sister."

"Very pleased to meet you. I'll be working with Anita."

"Yes." She nodded. "They come soon." She handed him his coffee and didn't want payment, so he put three dollars in the tip jar.

"Thank you, Claudia," he said, holding up his cup as he left. "See you tomorrow." He sipped his coffee on the way back to the station and made a face.

"Did she put cream and sugar?"

Anita surprised him, and he spilled a little. "Yes. I wasn't expecting that."

"Don't worry. I make great coffee. No one will drink it unless I make it." She unlocked the front door and began flipping on lights. "There was a call for you yesterday."

"For me? I hadn't even started yet."

"You know that lady you guys arrested, Holly Cooper? She wants to talk to you."

"I thought I might catch up with Jack at lunch for a progress report, so I can stop in and see her. How's Ernie?"

"He's doing better. Even the doctor is surprised."

"Good. When does Mick get in?"

"Usually eight or nine, depending on how late he was working the night before."

"No one's here at night?"

"Not usually, unless we're called in for an emergency."

Tom nodded.

"You worked in Las Vegas before, no?"

"Yes. I usually started my day at six."

"I guess you can sleep a little more now." She smiled. "If you want something to do, here are some papers they want you to fill out." She handed him a packet. "I'll go make some fresh coffee."

Tom spent the next hour filling out paperwork and drinking coffee, then he talked to Anita about the town and a typical day. Mick wandered in about nine and looked surprised to see him. "You didn't have to come in today, Tom. You just got back yesterday, and you're injured."

"I was scheduled for today, and I didn't call out. I'll always call out unless I'm dead or in a coma."

"Good to know. Want to take a little field trip to Las Rodillas? Anita told you Holly Cooper called?"

"Yes, I've been wondering what that's about."

"Let me grab a cup of coffee, and we'll head out."

"I might have one more too. I'm sorry I drank most of it, Anita. It really is delicious."

When they walked into the sheriff's station in Las Rodillas, Tom was surprised by how small it was because the town was considerably larger. Mick nodded to the receptionist and led Tom down a long hall to the cells.

"Don't we have to check in or something?"

"No. We all know each other here, and we're not letting her out of her cell." They walked a little farther and stopped at the last cell. "Holly, I brought Tom to talk to you."

Her head popped out from under a thin blanket. "Tom?"

"Yes, I'm here. What's going on?"

"Do we have to talk with the bars between us?"

"I'm afraid so. What did you want to talk about?"

"When we were up on the mountain, and Ernie and I were arguing, I didn't really understand what was going on, but something is really wrong, and I'm frightened."

"What do you mean?"

"I didn't kill Art. I didn't even know he was dead until you guys told me. I thought Ernie was messing with me. I wasn't too worried about it because I knew I hadn't done it, and I didn't have a different jacket. I hadn't been outside that night." She looked at Tom with pleading eyes. "Now, they are telling me there really was a small jacket and gloves with blood on them, and some guy claiming to be a witness. I think Ernie paid him to say it, maybe even to help, and if Ernie dies, he'll never be able to tell the truth."

Tom stared at her in disbelief. "You admitted to doing it."

"No, I didn't. Ernie said I did. What I said was that it wouldn't have happened if not for Sam. Ernie was covering for my brother. Art was getting in the way. I would never have killed Art. I loved him."

"Jack is doing the autopsies now. He'll be able to tell if you did it or not. I'll pass along your information, okay?"

"Thank you, Tom. No one else will listen to me."

He was in a daze when they left. "I'll have to go back through our notes. Can we go see Jack?"

"It's almost eleven. Why don't we just call him and ask him to meet us at Mary's? They don't always like to be interrupted."

"I'd prefer talking about this in private. Can you ask him?"

Mick called over, and Jack invited them to visit the morgue. He came out to greet them when they arrived and pointed at the cleansing station and box of gloves at the entry way. Despite the small sheriff's offices, the morgue was a large, up-to-date facility catering to examiners of Jack's caliber. Tom was impressed by the level of professionalism he beheld.

"To what do I owe the pleasure, gentlemen?""

"I'm sorry if we're interrupting. I asked Mick to call." Tom perched on a tall stool.

"Back still bothering you?"

"A little. It's not bad. Anyway, I just spoke with Holly, and she's concerned because she thinks Ernie set her up, and if he doesn't make it, his evidence will be lost."

"Do you believe her?"

"I think I do." Tom's brow furrowed. "That's why I wanted to talk to you."

"This has been an exceedingly difficult case because we were up there in the woods without any links to technology or proper evidence handling. Everyone was wearing gloves and hats, and we couldn't verify anyone's background. On top of that, the results from the tests I have been running have not been what I expected."

"What do you mean?"

"I tested David's statement and found that the knife couldn't have been inserted the way he said. The angle was wrong. So, I've been experimenting, trying to figure out how it went in. The only way I can find that would create that angle is if he was already lying face down. How would someone get him lying face down? Maybe by knocking him out? I started searching for a cranial contusion and found one on his right temple."

Mick stared at him. "Holly couldn't have hit him in the temple—"

"There's more. The jacket we brought in for evidence. The blood spatter is on the back, not the front. And the size is much too small for Holly. It's a child's jacket. Even though Holly is petite, she is very muscular. She wears a women's small, not a child's medium."

"You are saying that the murder was not committed by Holly," Tom said.

"I am saying that it's unlikely and that the evidence we have was manufactured."

"Based on what you have so far, can you tell if both murders could have been done by the same person?"

"I'm not sure yet. I'm also wondering if Ernie is intelligent enough to come up with the manufactured evidence or if he had help. That leads me to question David's testimony. Did he give a statement on what he thought he saw or was he paid to give a false statement? Or maybe he's the mastermind."

"Why would he lead us to Ernie if Ernie was paying him?" Mick asked.

"I'll keep working on this. Please don't let any information leak, and make sure to post guards on Ernie's room just in case. Ready for lunch?"

Tom followed Jack and Mick out of the room, disposing of his gloves and washing up at the sanitizing station. They crossed the street and walked down to Mary's.

When they entered, the server spotted Jack. "Welcome back! Your usual?"

"Thanks, Greta. I missed you too." He winked.

She sat them in the back corner booth and passed out menus. "Modelo Negra?"

"Yes, ma'am."

She raised her brows at Mick and Tom, who assented.

"It's good to be back for a while." Jack smiled.

"I heard you were on the brilliant scale, but today I'm convinced," Tom said.

"Oh, stop. You're already family. You don't have to pretend admiration."

"Okay, I'll pretend disdain, you hack."

Jack laughed. "I like you."

Greta returned with their beers and took their orders. It was still a little early, and they were able to converse without having to worry about eavesdropping.

"Sam and I met up here with her motorcycle friends when we drove back from Vegas. She ordered a Reuben."

"If given a choice, Sam will always order a Reuben, pizza, or barbecue."

Mick's mouth turned down at the corners, and he looked at his beer.

"Don't feel bad, old man. She didn't choose me either."

"You had a thing for her too?" Tom asked.

"Who wouldn't? She's so different, so full of life. Why did she pick you? I mean, you seem like a decent guy, but what makes you different?"

Tom shrugged. "I have no idea. I hadn't paid attention to a woman, any woman, for five years, then suddenly, Sam waltzed into my murder investigation, and it was like I was struck by lightning. She probably saved me from being that cranky old detective we all love to hate."

"There's no rhyme or reason, is there?" Jack said. "Love walks in and takes over. I don't think we really have a choice."

"You loved Alley," Mick said.

"Yeah, and she was murdered."

"Sorry. It's just that I don't have anyone to love. Sometimes I think I need to get out of Santo Milagro."

"Just have faith. The lightning will strike," Tom said. "I had lost all hope. I didn't even care anymore."

Greta returned with their food, and they discussed sports while they ate.

Mick and Tom said goodbye to Jack in the parking lot and headed back to Santo Milagro. When they got back, Mick told Tom to head home and that he'd get a call if he was needed.

Tom was looking forward to seeing Sam and pondering his luck on his drive home. It seemed like a lot of men were in the situation he was in, but somehow fate intervened when he met the woman of his dreams. He pulled into the drive and was surprised to see the blinds closed.

Entering the still house, he hollered, "Sam?" Chiquito sat on the table and stared at him. He ran up the stairs. "Sam?" He opened the door to their bedroom and found her lying in bed.

He took her temperature and called an ambulance.

Sitting on the edge of the bed, he took her hand. "Sam? Can you hear me?"

Her eyes flickered, and she gave him a small smile.

"What's wrong, Sam?"

"I don't know," she whispered. "I'm so tired, and I can't seem to get warm."

"Just hold on. I've called an ambulance. We'll get you to the hospital. I love you so much, Sam. Just hold on."

Chapter 18

Tom didn't sleep that night. He sat in a chair in the lobby, then in Sam's room, holding her hand and waiting to find out what was wrong with her. Mick, Roger, Melissa, and Anita all stopped by to see if there was anything they could do, but Tom still hadn't had any news. Jack stopped in to consult with the on-call doctor, but they couldn't tell him anything either.

Jack visited Sam's room and sat next to her bed. "Can you tell me how you are feeling?"

"I just can't seem to get warm, and I'm so tired. I got up this morning and took another hot bath, then crawled back into bed. I just wanted to feel warm."

"Can I take some of your blood and run some tests?"

"Yes. Thank you, Jack."

Jack got the paperwork in order and went to talk to Tom.

"I've seen your work, Jack. I'm grateful you're looking into it. I just want her to feel better."

"I'll figure it out. If they suggest any extreme treatments, tell them to wait. I'll call you as soon as I figure it out."

Jack took the samples and drove back to Las Rodillas. He worked all night and called Tom in the morning. "It's anemia. We can get her on iron supplements. I'll be there in an hour."

Tom hung up and held onto Sam's hand as he said a prayer of gratitude.

When Jack arrived, he consulted with the on-call doctor again and accompanied him to Sam's room. They gave her a shot, and Jack stayed with Tom. "Sometimes the simplest solution is the most effective. She'll be fine. Her exposure to the cold and her unbalanced meals exacerbated her anemia."

143

Tom held on to Jack's hand. He bit his bottom lip hard as he tried to stop his tears. "Thanks," he choked out. "She's my world. I don't think I could go on without her." He bit harder, blinking rapidly, and took a deep breath. "I don't know how to explain it to you, but she saved my life. I need her."

Jack, not a demonstrative man, hugged Tom hard. "I understand. She'll be fine." He whacked him twice on the shoulder and let go. "Sit with her until she wakes. She'll be fine." He nodded and left the room before he embarrassed himself.

He went out to his car and sat for a few minutes. He thought about Tom and how much he loved and needed Sam. Even though he craved that kind of love, he found it terrifying. *What would happen if you lost that? Is that what my father felt?* He shook that thought from his mind and drove back to the morgue.

Tom sat by Sam's bed after Jack left. He held onto her hand, and he prayed. He meant what he said to Jack. Sam had saved him from a hardened heart and a life of nothing more than work. *Please, Lord, help her be okay. You sent her to me when I needed her most. Please don't take her away.*

Sam got well quickly once they figured out what was ailing her. She was still happy to stay snuggled up in bed, but once Tom told her about Holly's concern and Jack's test results, she was anxious to get up and take action. "Drive me to the morgue, Tom," she said as they were still processing her discharge paperwork. Once they were in the car, she said, "Tell me again what Holly said to you in the jail." Tom did his best to repeat exactly what she said, and Sam stared at him. "She said Ernie was covering for her brother? I thought Ernie was her brother. We need to have Mick check into their family."

"Can you call him now?"

Sam dialed the station and asked Anita to speak with Mick. "I'm sorry, Sam, he's not here. He left for the morgue about an hour ago.

"Thanks, Anita. I'll call him there."

She hung up and called Jack, but he didn't answer. Thoroughly frustrated, Sam sat back and blew air out of her nose.

"We'll be there soon." Tom smiled.

Just as they pulled into the morgue parking lot, Jack returned Sam's call. "Jack! Where are you?"

"I'm at Mary's with Mick. Why don't you join us? I see your truck."

"On our way."

She and Tom got out of the truck and were hit by an icy blast of air. Sam shivered, and Tom raced around the truck to bundle her up. "I'm okay now, Tom. You don't have to coddle me." She smiled.

"You're not cold?"

"Of course I am, but that's normal in this wind. Let's get inside."

They hurried into Mary's and joined Jack and Mick in the back booth.

"Kind of déjà vu, huh. Am I allowed to have a Modelo, doc?"

"I think you deserve it."

"Yay!"

Greta approached the table and said, "The gang's all here. A Reuben and a Modelo Negra?"

"Yes, ma'am. Good to see you, Greta."

"I guess I'll have the same," Tom said.

Greta nodded and left the table to put in the order.

"I have news."

She told Jack and Mick about Holly's words to Tom and suggested Mick have someone research the Cooper family.

"I was standing right there. How did I miss that?"

"I missed it too."

"I'll be right back. I need to make a call." Mick left the table and went outside just as Greta was returning with his order.

"Is he leaving?"

"No, he'll be back. Thanks." Jack took his plate.

"What is that? It smells good."

"Yours is coming. Leave mine alone."

Sam pouted.

"Fine. You can have a bite. It's the special ham and mashed potatoes with red sauce."

"Mmm." Sam swiped a bite of potatoes. "Not as good as a Reuben, but almost."

Mick returned to the table and took a mouthful of his fried chicken.

"You should have driven faster, Tom."

"I know. I'm sorry." He couldn't quite hide his smile.

Greta chose that moment to bring the Reubens, and Sam smiled and popped a tater tot in her mouth.

"I would like to say your stay in the cave changed you," Jack said, "but you've always enjoyed your food."

"I have a new appreciation for Ben, though. That survival food was terrible. I don't ever want to stay outside without proper food again." She took a big bite of her sandwich.

"You did an excellent job of planning. We didn't run out of food, even with the extended stay."

"That might have been partly because Sam wasn't there to eat it." Jack grinned.

"Hey! Why're you picking on me?"

"Because I can."

She stuck her tongue out at him and took another bite of her sandwich.

Tom smiled, watching them act like siblings. His relationship with Sam was different, and he wasn't jealous anymore. He could see the way they interacted and Sam's happy, easy relationship with her cousin. Jack told him that Sam made friends easily, but he was pleased that she had so many life-long friends she could trust and rely on. The time she spent in Vegas must have been hard, getting thrown into a murder investigation without her support system.

"Hey," she said, leaning up against him. "Everything okay?"

"Yes, everything is just fine." He kissed her temple and smiled at her.

When they finished lunch, they walked back to the morgue. Jack showed Tom and Sam what he'd been working on, and Mick looked at his e-mail.

"I have an update," he said. "Holly and Ernie are cousins. Her brother's name is…."

"David Cooper?" Sam asked.

"How did you know that?"

"Who was our star witness?"

"David Arndt," Tom said.

"Who told us about the mail drop, the swapped jacket and gloves, and how Holly killed Art?"

"David Arndt," Jack said.

"And who did Art tell us was very dangerous and a killer?"

"Holly's brother," said Tom.

"He didn't say Ernie; he said Holly's brother. She didn't understand what was going on. Her brother was using Ernie to frame her, but Art said he would do anything for her. She trusted him and didn't give him away."

"How are we going to find him?" Jack asked. "Everything he told us was a lie."

"Not everything. We just have to figure out which things he was lying about. Does he have a grandmother? Maybe he really is living with her. Does he have social media accounts? Is the hunting group in his name or in Ernie's? We need to hunt him down with the clues he gave us."

Mick was taking notes.

"By the way, we need to check on Art's dog, Bear. He's probably locked in the house and might have run out of food and water. Does he have a legal contact? Maybe we can ask Holly?"

"Do you want to come over to the sheriff's office with me and talk to her?"

"Yes. I think I should."

Mick sent an e-mail response and left the morgue with Sam. "I'll be back soon."

He took Sam to the Sheriff's station and down the hall he had traversed with Tom, calling out to Holly. "I have Sam here to talk to you."

Holly glared at Sam. "What do you want?"

"Tom told me about your conversation, and I wanted to ask you about your brother."

"That was private. He shouldn't have blabbed it to you. It's none of your business."

"Holly, listen to me, please. You told Tom that Ernie was covering for your brother. We thought Ernie was your brother."

"What? Why? He's my cousin."

"Art didn't mention names, and we didn't know two different men were involved. What is your brother's name?"

"His name is David. He was there in the tent with us. He was your witness?"

Sam nodded. "He's the one who told us you killed Art."

Holly stared at her in shock. "I trusted him. He set me up?"

"It looks like it. The jacket they put in the blind was too small for you, and most of the blood spatter was on the back. He must have put his arms in the jacket from the front."

Holly groaned and seemed to deflate before Sam's eyes. "I owe you a big apology. I thought you were out to ruin my life, and it turns out you are the only one looking out for me."

"I just want to find out the truth, and when Tom told me you said Ernie was looking out for your brother, I had to stop and think about that. Art was an amazing instructor, and he was trying to help me up there on the mountain. He loved you and didn't think you would harm him, and he was right. Let's get the real bad guy behind bars."

"Thanks, Sam. I appreciate your help. I knew David was evil when he killed Scott, but I never would have thought him capable of killing Art and then framing me for it."

"We're working on it, Holly. And by the way, I'm worried about Bear.

Do you know who Art had caring for him or an attorney or family member we might contact?"

"Try Bardwell and Salomon here in town. They might know what to do."

"Thanks. I'll keep you informed."

150

Chapter 19

Sam left the sheriff's office with Mick and placed a call to Bardwell and Salomon. They walked down Main Street to the legal offices, and Mick waited in the lobby while she met with Mr. Bardwell. His office was modest, with one large desk, two visitor's chairs, and rows of bookshelves.

He stood when she entered and shook her hand. "Hello, Ms. Olivares. Thank you for coming in." He sat behind his desk and gestured for her to sit as well. "How can I be of assistance?"

"It's Mrs. Cork now. I heard from Art's girlfriend, Holly Cooper, that I should contact you regarding his dog, Bear. Art was killed recently, and I'm worried that Bear is locked in his house without food and water. Is there someone I can contact to make sure he is taken care of?"

Mr. Bardwell raised his eyebrows. "That is your only concern?"

"Well, yes. It occurred to me that he might not have made long-term arrangements for Bear, and I know he cared about him a great deal. Would it be possible for me to take him into temporary custody?"

"Temporary custody?" He cleared his throat.

"Has someone been assigned to care for him?"

"Ms. er Mrs. Cork, you are the sole heir to Mr. Jimenez's estate. Everything he owned, including his dog Bear, has been bequeathed to you."

"What? No. That's quite impossible."

"I assure you; it is a fact."

"But even if that's so, probate can take a long time. We need to do something about Bear." Sam, eyes wide, was beginning to panic.

"I can have one of our paralegals accompany you to his home to retrieve the dog. A living being is not subject to probate."

Sam relaxed. "Thank goodness. Do you have a note or anything from Art? I'm sure he wouldn't want me to ignore his partner's claims to his business, and he must have some instructions for me."

"We will have a reading of the will and instructions at a later date. I was just trying to allay your fears as to the canine in question."

"Yes, thank you very much. Can your paralegal accompany me to his home right away?"

After saying goodbye to Mick, Sam followed Mr. Berry, a paralegal for Bardwell and Salomon, to Art's home. When Mr. Berry unlocked the kitchen door, Bear came charging out like he was escaping a life sentence in a primitive dungeon. Recognizing Sam, he stopped momentarily to sniff her hand before racing around the property at top speed. Sam went inside to check Bear's food and water, which had run out. She refilled his bowls and took them outside for him. Bear stopped his galivanting for a few minutes to eat, then began to run again.

"What should I do about him, Mr. Berry? Should I take him home for now or leave him here?"

"According to the will, you are his caretaker."

"I don't even know if he'll get along with the other dog or the horses."

"Since he is alone here, I imagine it will be better if he is with someone who cares about him."

"I suppose so. He is such an amazing dog. I can't imagine why Art didn't discuss this with me ahead of time."

"Most people don't think anything is going to happen to them when they make a will. He probably made it as a precaution and then...."

"Yes. You're right. Art was confident in his abilities. I'm sure he never imagined anything would happen to him.

Bear knows me because I was over here every day, training for my survival certification."

"Why don't you see if you can get him into your truck, and if you can, we'll load up his food and lock the door to the house."

"Bear! Let's go, boy. Hop on in." Bear bounded into the truck and sat, panting on the front seat. "Good boy. Let me just get your food, and we'll go for a ride."

Sam thanked Mr. Berry and drove home. She asked Bear to wait and got out of the truck to speak with Roger.

"I don't have a collar and leash for him, and I don't know how he reacts around other dogs. What should we do?"

"Red minds, so let's just see what happens."

Sam let Bear out and set his food and water bowl down. Bear approached Red and sniffed him, then he ran around the yard checking everything out.

Red sat quietly. Finally, Bear ran over to Red and sat beside him. They touched noses and waited together, watching Roger and Sam.

Sam looked at Roger. "Do you want him to be your dog or mine? I have the cats."

"I'll see how they get along if you like. He seems to like Red."

Sam nodded. "If he doesn't work out, we'll try something else.

Roger whistled to Red, and Bear followed.

Sam went to visit Antoine and kept an eye on the dogs. Antoine, her black and white ornamental turkey, was always ecstatic to see her. Even though she made sure he was taken care of, he was partial to Sam and expected her to visit him every day. He ran out to greet her and settled himself on her lap, where he expected plenty of pets and adoration. "Hello, pretty boy," Sam cooed. "Did you miss me? Were you a good boy while I was gone?" Antoine gobbled and pressed against her. "Poor baby. I'm sorry I was gone so long. Do you want a piece of apple?" Sam gave him a little treat and lots of pets to make up for her absence. When he seemed appeased, she said goodbye and went back into the house. She wondered how long it would take for Bear to get used to the turkey.

Tom had stayed in Las Rodillas with Jack and arrived home with trepidation. The last time, he found Sam in need of medical attention. This time she was in the kitchen, cooking lasagna. It smelled so good; he stopped and inhaled the rich scent before walking up behind her. "Aren't you supposed to be resting?"

"Resting is good. Lasagna is better." Sam smiled when he nuzzled her ear.

"Lasagna is good, but a rested, healthy wife is better."

"Let's eat some yummy lasagna and then rest together."

"Hard to argue with that."

"It's almost ready." She wrapped her arms around his neck and kissed him soundly.

"I'm ready to give up the lasagna for some more of those kisses."

"Nooo. I worked hard on this. You must love the lasagna."

"It smells almost as good as you do."

"Go take a shower, and it will be ready."

He tore himself away and went to take his shower. When he returned, she was taking it out of the oven and shooing Jack off to take his shower.

She dished out the lasagna, salad, and garlic bread when they reconvened and waited until everyone had taken a bite before asking about the case.

"Ernie doesn't have any siblings," Jack said. "And Holly's brother David has been a person of interest numerous times but always got off on a technicality."

"Is he the same David? Have you seen any pictures?"

"It's him, and his address on file is his grandmother's home. His social media accounts have a lot of hunting pictures, including one with Kevin and a group of men sitting around a fire." Tom rubbed his chin.

"Kevin didn't recognize David at the camp." Sam tilted her head.

"Kevin was pretty out of it at first. I'm not sure he really looked at him. Plus, in his mind, Ernie was the bad guy.

Can I have seconds?" Jack got up and took his plate to the stove.

Sam nodded absentmindedly. "So, Holly said her brother killed Scott, but then Ernie took the fall for that, saying it was self-defense, and both of them denied killing Art."

Jack and Tom nodded.

"When Holly left the blind, Ernie said, 'Holly be reasonable.' What do you think they were fighting about?"

"I forgot about that." Jack took another bite of lasagna.

"Art told us that he knew it was Holly's brother out there with Scott, and he said that he didn't think Holly would harm him, but her brother was a killer. He never mentioned Ernie by name. Did he know Ernie was helping David?"

"Ernie doesn't seem like the brightest bulb," Jack said.

"I missed so much, being stuck in the sick bay."

"How are those stitches healing?"

"They're itching."

"I'll need to take them out at some point. Did they stitch you up while you were in the hospital, Sam?"

"Yeah, I'm good. Did they check Ernie for a bullet wound?"

"He didn't have one. I bet I know who does." Tom set his fork on his empty plate. "That was delicious, Sam."

"I think I might explode." Jack put his fork down, too, and leaned back with his hands on his stomach.

Sam smiled but then frowned when she thought about Holly. "Are the police looking for David?"

"Yes. Let's make sure the house is locked up tonight since we don't know where he is or how much he's heard."

"There's a guard at the hospital with Ernie?"

"Yes. I'll warn Roger, too." Jack stood and put on his coat. "Leave the dishes for me. I'll take care of them."

"Thanks, Jack."

He gave her a little wave as he left. He was thinking about her and Tom, settled and homey at the ranch when he heard a low growl.

He looked around, alarmed at the alien sound, and jerked backward when David was suddenly standing in his path holding a knife. "Was that you?" Jack asked.

"Was what me?"

"That sound."

"I don't know what you're talking about, but we need to have a little conversation."

"About what? Did you forget something at the camp?"

Jack heard it again, that low growl.

"Don't play dumb with me. I know you figured it out, and now you need to forget it."

"I wasn't the one who figured it out, but the entire sheriff's office knows now, so even if I forget it, no one else will."

"We'll see about that. Let's go for a ride."

"I don't think so."

Jack stepped back as a large ball of white charged from the barn and knocked David on his back. He tried to stab the white monster, but it grabbed his wrist with its teeth.

"Augh," he yelled. "Get it off me."

"Good boy, Bear," Roger said, running toward them. "I've called the sheriff's office. Mick's on his way."

"Did you get a new dog?" Jack asked shakily.

"Naw. This is Art's dog, now mine, it seems. He likes Red."

"I heard him growl."

"Me too, huh."

Mick pulled in with his lights flashing, and Sam and Tom came out of the house to see what was happening. Bear was still sitting on David, who was too terrified to move. When Mick approached, Bear looked at Roger, who nodded, so he got up and went to sit next to Red.

"I need medical attention," David yelled. "That thing probably gave me rabies. I demand to be taken to the hospital."

"You have the right to remain silent...."

Mick began the Miranda warning while cuffing him and helping him into the back seat of his cruiser. He locked the door and returned to the small group. "Is anyone injured?"

"No, Bear saved me," Jack said. "You might want to bag his knife."

Mick pulled out a bag and picked up the knife. "If you decide you don't want him, I could use a good police dog."

"You might be disappointed. Roger is a dog whisperer, and I suspect he helped Art train him." Sam looked at Roger.

Roger ducked his head and shrugged. "I might have given him a hand."

"Ha. I thought so."

"I'll take the suspect to Las Rodillas and have a deputy available to take notes when he and his sister decide to speak. See you tomorrow morning, Tom."

"Yes, sir."

"You do know I'm not your boss, right?"

"Yes, I know." Tom smiled.

"Okay, then." Mick returned to his cruiser and drove away.

"That was crazy," Jack said. "Did you see that, Roger?"

"Yes, I did. Bear has already earned his keep, no?"

Sam looked from one to the other. "What happened?"

"You go ahead and tell her. I'm going to finish up in the barn."

"Thanks, Roger. Thank you, Bear." Jack watched the man and his two faithful companions walk toward the barn, then he turned back to Sam and Tom. "Let's go back in the house, and I'll tell you the story. Do you still have that bottle, Sam?"

"Maybe not that one, but I'm sure I can scrounge something up."

"You look shaken," Tom said.

He and Jack sat at the kitchen table.

"David popped up out of nowhere, but before he did, I heard this frightening growl, so I was already nervous."

"What did he want?" Sam brought three glasses and a bottle of Canadian Club and sat them on the kitchen table.

Tom poured and handed Jack a glass.

"He said he knew I'd figured it out, and now I had to forget it. When I told him everyone knew, he wanted me to go somewhere with him. Does he have a vehicle here?"

Tom shook his head. "I don't know. I didn't see one."

"Anyway, I heard that growl again, but he didn't seem to hear it, and when I took a step back, Bear went flying at him and knocked him down. I didn't even know what that great, furry beast was. He was terrifying, and he saved me." Jack's hand shook slightly as he sipped from his glass.

Sam thought about her friend Marcus from Las Vegas. "Marcus sure loved Bear, but I don't think he would know what to do with him." Sam took a sip and shuddered.

"Not much of a whiskey drinker, huh?"

"Not unless I'm freezing on the side of a mountain. Let me see if we've got some coke." She got up and rummaged in the refrigerator, returning triumphant.

Tom shook his head, and Jack ignored her. "Did you know about this, Jack?"

"Of course." His lips turned up slightly.

"About what?" Sam sat down and poured the coke into her glass. "We should get some sleep. You two have work in the morning, and I want to find out what's happening at the jail."

She put the bottle away, and they finished their drinks before heading upstairs.

Chapter 20

The next morning, Sam woke early to the smell of coffee and pancakes. She looked over at Tom and smiled. Amazing. He's still sleeping. He must have been tired. Getting dressed quickly, she skipped down the stairs to find Jack making breakfast.

He looked at her and laughed. Her hair was mushed on one side and sprouting like a plant on the other. "I like the red better," he said.

"Me too, but the blue did match my bike."

"Priorities," they said together and laughed.

Jack handed her a cup of coffee and set a plate of pancakes on the table.

She was about to take a pancake when Tom wandered downstairs in his pajamas.

"You guys belong together." Jack eyed Tom's hair.

Tom looked at Sam, confused.

"He's making fun of our bedheads."

"Yours is pretty funny."

"Have you looked in the mirror?"

He laughed and gave her a kiss on the cheek. "Any more coffee?"

"You can have a little, but the rest is mine."

"We'd better make some more for our own personal safety." Jack raised an eyebrow.

"Can I ride in with you today?" Sam smeared butter and jam on her pancake, added some homemade applesauce, then drizzled natural maple syrup on the top.

"Maybe you can bring your truck in case you want to leave since I'll be working all day."

"But I can leave it in Santo Milagro when we drive to Las Rodillas?"

"Why are we driving to Las Rodillas?"

Sam stared at him. "To talk to Holly."

"We might not need to. It depends on what happened last night. Mick will give us an update when we get to the station."

"Aren't you late?"

"I found out that no one shows up until eight or nine. Anita told me I can sleep more."

Sam laughed. "The perks of living in the country."

She washed the dishes, fed the cats, combed her hair, and went out to see Antoine while Tom got ready for work. Roger came out with Bear, who sniffed at the turkey shelter and licked Sam's hand before returning to sit next to Roger. "How's he doing?"

Roger looked down and put his hand on Bear's head. "He's doing remarkably well, considering his owner is missing, and he's in a strange place."

"Poor thing. I'm glad he remembers you."

"The ranch will be a good place for him to get plenty of exercise and be around lots of people and animals, huh."

"I have to go now," she said, glancing toward the house when Tom and Jack came outside. "I'll check in when I get back." She scratched Bear's head and gave Roger a little wave before trotting toward her truck.

She followed Tom into town and waved at Jack when he continued toward the morgue, then she parked in front of the station. Pushing through the glass doors and looking around for Tom and Mick, Sam said, "Hello, Anita."

"Hi, Sam. They're back in Captain Blatt's office. You might want to wait here."

Sam frowned, but she sat on the bench along the front window, knowing that the captain was a stickler for protocol and wouldn't likely welcome her intrusion. She waited for quite a while until Tom came out to talk to her.

"Mick and I convinced the captain that you should speak with Holly. She and David completely ignored each other when he was brought in."

"They seem to have some kind of agreement, which is strange since he and Ernie framed her for Art's murder. How is Ernie, by the way?"

"He's awake but isn't going anywhere. He has a lot of broken bones."

"Can we talk to him?"

"Let me suggest that we stop at the hospital first. I'll be back in a few minutes."

Sam remained on the bench.

"The captain told me that you should just join the sheriff's department since you always seem involved in our cases anyway."

Sam looked up with surprise.

"He doesn't mind your help. He just likes to follow protocol." Anita smiled.

"Mick said that before, but I wouldn't like sitting behind a desk or answering phones all the time."

"That is part of the job." Anita nodded.

Sam stood as Tom and Mick approached her, followed by Captain Blatt. "Good to see you, Sam. I hear you'll be speaking with our suspects this afternoon."

"Thank you for allowing me to assist, captain."

"You know the drill. Just make sure to let Tom and Mick do their jobs."

"Yes, sir. I will." She shook his hand and left the station with Mick and Tom. They took Mick's cruiser to the hospital at the other end of Main Street.

It was a small, two-story building, more like a clinic than a hospital, with enough beds for emergency patients, a small maternity ward, surgeries, and post-op patients. Ernie was in a private room on the second floor, with a guard posted outside his door. The guard checked Mick's ID and let them pass.

"Hello, Ernie," Tom said when they entered.

"Who are you?" he squinted at the trio.

"We were part of the camping group on the mountain. I'm Detective Thomas Cork, and I believe you know Sergeant Mickelson."

"Yes, we're acquainted," he said with a sneer.

"This is Sam, the lady you were trying to get rid of, I believe."

"Yeah, funny. You're still here, and I'm in the hospital."

"Running headlong into a snowcat isn't good for your health."

He glared at Mick. "Not like I did it on purpose."

"Why didn't you tell us about David? He was sitting right there in the tent with you," Sam said.

"David, who?"

"Cooper. Holly's brother. He's letting you take the fall for him. Why are you protecting him?"

"I don't know what you're talking about."

"So, you stand by your statement that you killed Scott, and you aided and abetted Holly when she killed Art?" Sam asked. "You do understand that you'll be in prison for the rest of your life."

Ernie just stared at her and said nothing.

Sam shrugged. "I just hope Holly is smarter than you are."

"You leave Holly alone."

"So she can spend life in prison for something she didn't do?" Sam turned and left the room.

"That's cold, Ernie," Mick said before he and Tom followed Sam out.

"I hope Holly isn't that stubborn. What do you think David has on them?" Sam asked when they met outside.

"I have no idea. What could be worse than murder?" Tom said.

"Let's see if we can find out."

The ride to Las Rodillas was a silent one, but when they approached the town limits, Tom said, "We should talk to her in one of the interview rooms so David can't interfere."

"I agree. Do you want to be alone with her first, Sam?"

"I wonder if she'd rather talk to Tom. She likes you."

"Maybe. Why don't I give it a try."

Mick checked them in and asked to speak with Holly. He and Sam stood behind the one-way glass, and Tom sat at the interview table to wait. The room was white and bare except for the table and three plastic chairs.

A deputy brought Holly in and handcuffed her to the table. "Just holler if you need me," he said on his way out.

Holly smiled at Tom. "I'm glad to see you. Who do you have with you?" She pointed at the glass.

"Sam's with me, but I thought you might prefer to speak in private. Have you spoken with an attorney?"

"No, not yet."

"You didn't kill anyone, did you."

Holly looked at him with wide eyes. "You believe me?"

"I do, but I don't understand why you didn't tell us about David."

"My brother? I told you he killed Scott."

"But we thought Ernie was your brother, and then he admitted to killing Scott."

Holly sighed. "I thought David had my back. I trusted him with my life, but he was just trying to protect his hunting business. I can't believe he set me up, but Ernie is too stupid to come up with that kind of plan."

"Art warned us about your brother, but he never used his name. Why didn't you acknowledge him when you were being questioned in the second tent?"

"I thought Ernie was making things up and David was going to help me."

"You didn't say anything to him when he was brought in last night."

"I may never speak to him again. He took Art away from me and then made sure I was blamed for it. What kind of brother does that? I miss Art so much." Her head dropped, and her shoulders quaked.

Tom sat quietly and waited, trying to imagine Holly's profound grief.

"She looked up with red eyes and hiccupped. Where is Bear? Art loved that dog more than anything."

"Art left him to Sam. He's at the ranch."

"Oh, good. I could never handle him. He only ever listened to Art." Holly sniffed, and her tears clung to her lashes. "Art and our business were all I had. I don't know how to go on without him."

"The first step is to get you out of here. I need any information you can give me that will help exonerate you."

"I witnessed David stab Scott, but I don't know how to help with Art's murder because I wasn't there."

"Was there anyone awake during the night who might be able to give you an alibi?"

"I don't know. I didn't wake until Sissy started screaming."

"Did you find any of your belongings rearranged or missing?"

Holly's eyes rolled up as she thought. "My boots were by the tent flap, and they were wet. I'm pretty sure I left them by my cot after I visited the outhouse, and they should have been dry by morning."

"Anything else?"

"When we had the carving lesson, my knife wasn't where I put it in my pack."

"I don't think that was your pack. You were looking in Sissy's pack."

"Oh. Then I guess that's not where I put it." Her lips turned up slightly.

"Whose idea was the sabotage?"

"That was my idea." She looked down. "I'm sorry about that."

"And the arrows?"

"David told me I should use them to scare Sam, but when I missed, he grabbed my bow and shot you. Then Sam started shooting at us, and he told Ernie to go take care of her and said we had to get back to camp."

"You didn't see Art?"

Holly shook her head. "Art was a phantom. No one saw him unless he wanted them to. I didn't know he was there."

"Did you know anything about Lisa and her fiancé?"

"Was he at the camp?"

"No, she was looking for him."

Holly shook her head. "She didn't confide in me."

"Thank you. Your information should help us sort this out."

"Just don't put David and me in the same room because one of us won't be leaving."

"I understand. I'll be back to see you again."

"Thank you for believing me, Tom. I won't forget it."

Tom knocked on the door, and the deputy took Holly back to her cell.

She turned as they left and said, "Tell Sam I said hi."

Mick and Sam joined Tom in the interview room and sat at the table with him.

"That was exhausting," he said.

Sam rubbed his back gently. "Has anyone interviewed David?"

"We tried last night, but he wasn't talking."

"I imagine he has a lawyer," Tom said.

"He hasn't asked for one. He hasn't said a word."

"Is the deputy still stationed outside their cells? He might have something to say since she's been interviewed." Sam got up and paced. "Let's go talk to Jack and see if he's found anything else. Then maybe we can try Ernie again."

"You don't think we should talk to David?" Mick asked.

"I think you should have all your ducks in a row before you tackle him. He's going to be tough to crack. You might even want Jack with you."

"Okay. Let's walk over to the morgue. Maybe he'll have lunch with us again." Mick smiled and waggled his eyebrows.

They walked to the morgue, and Jack came out to greet them.

He led them along the long, clinical-looking hallway to his regular examination room. Jack had everything put away during Tom's previous visit. This time he had both bodies out and side by side on two tables. He had charts and graphs up on the electronic monitors and myriad tools lying on trays and tables and soaking in bowls.

"Have you discovered anything new?" Mick asked.

"The knife that killed Art might have been the same one that killed Scott. I didn't think so originally, but given the angle, it went in and the fact that it wasn't twisted, it's even possible that it was done by the same person."

"Holly said her boots were moved and were wet in the morning, but she didn't wake once she went to bed."

"That could account for the small, deep prints next to Art's body."

"One thing that puzzles me Holly said that David sent Ernie after me and that the two of them returned to camp, but just before I ran, I threw a rock into some bushes, and someone shot an arrow at me. Ernie said he only used a gun."

"He might have been lying. The arrows we found in the blind don't match the arrow that shot Tom. There may have been more than one bow and quivers."

Sam perched on the edge of a stool. "It's so hard to figure out who is telling the truth. We should go talk to Ernie again."

"Why don't we have some lunch first. Is anyone else hungry?"

"Me." Mick raised his hand and grinned.

"Lunch first, then. I need to put a few things away. I'll meet you in the lobby."

They all washed up and waited for Jack before heading to Mary's.

Chapter 21

Back in Santo Milagro, after a hearty lunch, Mick dropped Sam off at her truck and continued to the hospital with Tom. When they arrived at Ernie's room, he was yelling at the orderlies and threw his tray of food at the door, just missing Mick as he entered. "What's going on, Ernie?" he asked. "The accommodations here are too nice for your taste? You'd rather be in the prison sick bay?"

"Get. Out. No one gives me any privacy."

"Prisoners don't get privacy. You've been to jail before. You know how it works."

"I didn't even do anything."

Mick sat in a folding chair while Tom remained by the door.

"I'm aware of that, Ernie, but to make sure the murderer spends time in jail instead of you, we need you to cooperate."

"I can't."

"Yes, you can. Holly did. She told us she saw David kill Scott, and she told us that you weren't smart enough to plan Art's murder. All you need to do is tell us what happened."

"He'll kill me."

"How will he kill you from jail?"

"I don't know, but he will."

"How many other times have you gone to jail because you were covering for him?"

"Every time. He gives me work, gets me into trouble, and leaves me hanging."

"So why do you put up with it? He's destroying your life."

"He is my life. Without him, I don't have friends or a job or a roof over my head."

"Ernie, you need to make a decision. If you go to jail for this, you will never get out. Your life on the outside will be over. He doesn't care. He set up his own sister."

"That surprised me. He's changed."

"Did he tell you why?"

"He said Art would ruin our hunting business."

Mick leaned forward. "Is it your hunting business? Are you a partner?"

"No. Just his."

"And why frame Holly? What did she do to him?"

"She told him to leave Art alone. She told him if he hurt Art, she would kill him."

"So, he figured out a way to make sure she couldn't."

"I guess so."

"Do you want Holly to go to jail for something she didn't do?"

"No." Ernie hung his head.

"Do you want to go to prison again for something you didn't do?"

He shook his head.

"Tell me what happened to Art."

Ernie sighed. "David tricked me. He sent me a note in Holly's drop box. He said to come to camp with the small coat and gloves in the blind and to meet him behind the outhouse at two in the morning."

"Do you still have the note?"

"I don't know. It might be in one of my pockets."

Mick nodded. "What happened when you got there?"

"He took the coat and gloves and sent me to tell Art that Holly wanted to see him."

"You knew Art?"

"Well, yeah. He came to family dinners and stuff."

"So, he didn't suspect anything."

"I don't think so. We walked between the tents, and when we came out, David hit him on the head with something, and he fell."

"Was he unconscious?"

"I don't know. David moved so fast. He stood with his feet under Art's arms, facing the same direction, and stabbed him. He was holding the knife with both hands, and blood sprayed all over the little coat and gloves. He stood up straight and backed away, wiping his footprints, then took a small pair of boots, put his hands inside, and punched the snow with them."

"Where did he punch the snow?"

"Next to Art, by his hand. Then he told me to go back to the blind and gave me the jacket and gloves. 'I'll see you tomorrow,' he said, and that was the last time I saw him until those campers came and got me."

"What were you and Holly arguing about at the blind? You said, 'Holly, be reasonable.'"

"She was yelling at me about killing Art."

"Did you understand David's statement?"

Ernie shook his head.

"He said he witnessed Art's murder, that Holly killed him and handed you her bloody jacket."

"He's a devil," Ernie said with wide eyes. "No wonder granny doesn't trust him. She calls him the Cooper hawk."

"Does she trust you, Ernie?"

"Yeah. I don't know why since I keep going to jail."

"Some people are a good judge of character." Mick put his hand on Ernie's shoulder. "Thank you for your help. I hope you'll get well soon."

"Thanks, man." Ernie nodded. "Tell Holly I'm sorry."

"Good stuff," Tom said once they were outside. "Let's go visit his granny."

Mick nodded and unlocked the cruiser. "Sam's making the rounds." He nodded toward the other end of Main Street, where she was walking into a shop.

"What are the rounds?"

"She's walking around town saying hello to her friends. You can ask her about it tonight." He smiled.

"Do you know where the grandmother lives?"

"Yes, I know her. She lives a ways outside of town. Buckle up for a bumpy ride."

"Maybe we should take a truck."

"No, that'll just scare her. She knows the cruiser."

"So many things for me to learn."

"You'll figure them out. You're a quick study."

They bounced along the dirt road to the ranch but kept going, turning left, and following the river before turning left again on an even bumpier road filled with large potholes camouflaged by lingering snow. By the time they got to their destination, Tom was feeling a little sick.

Mick pulled up to a small, adobe-style house decorated with large potted plants covered in plastic and hanging wind chimes. They got out of the cruiser, and the front door opened before they reached the porch. A tiny woman with a large gray bun and pink-framed glasses peeked out of the doorway. "Sergeant. This is a pleasant surprise. Who's your friend?"

"Hello, Mrs. Cooper. This is Detective Cork. He's new to our team."

"A detective! Welcome. Would you like some tea?"

Tom was about to decline when Mick accepted for both of them. "That would be great. Thank you. Do you have any of those special little cookies you make?"

"You know I do, dear. I keep them just for you." Seeing her big smile made Tom understand why Mick accepted. *I have to remember that this isn't the big city.*

"Go ahead and have a seat on the sofa. I'll be right there."

Mick rose and helped her with the tray when she was ready, and she sat across from them on her antique love seat. She poured their tea and handed them each a cup.

Tom took a sip of his tea and a bite of cookie. "These are delicious. What are they?"

"Those are bizcochitos. Haven't you had them before?"

"I had some during the holidays, but these taste a little different. Do you have a secret ingredient?"

"Oh, yes, dear. Everyone who makes them adds their own special touch."

"Well, these are excellent."

"I know you boys are here on business. Which one is it this time?"

"Actually, I just wanted to ask you something." Mick set his teacup gently on a coaster. "I was talking to Ernie earlier today, and he told me that you don't really trust David. Then I asked him if you trusted him, Ernie, and he said he thinks so, even though he's been in and out of prison so many times."

Mrs. Cooper smiled a little and nodded. "Ernie is not extremely bright, but he's perceptive."

"Could you tell me a little bit about that? About what Ernie told us?"

"They are family, you understand, but sometimes a person can tell when something or someone is not quite right. David... he makes me nervous sometimes. He lies, and he's violent, not toward me, but I've seen him get very angry with other people. I think he uses Ernie a lot, but Ernie never complains."

"How about Holly?"

"She's a lovely girl, even if I don't quite understand her fashion or her occupation. She looks after the boys and tries to bail them out of trouble when she can." She looked at Mick sharply. "Has something happened?"

"Yes, but I'm not at liberty to say too much right now. You've been a very big help."

Mrs. Cooper's chin quivered a little. "Are they all okay? I haven't seen them for over a week."

"They are all safe. I'll come back with more information as soon as I can."

"Thank you, dear."

"Thank you for the tea and cookies." Mick smiled.

"Don't forget, please."

"I won't. I'll see you again soon."

As they drove away, the last thing Tom saw was her waving goodbye from the porch. He sat silent, lost in thought, on the way back to town. Finally, he looked at Mick and said, "It's gut-wrenching. She seems like such a genuinely kind lady."

"Maybe we can fix it a little if we can get the correct grandson behind bars."

Tom beat Jack back to the ranch and found Sam in the living room, reading a book with the cats. Chiquito was draped around her shoulders, and Preciosa was on her lap. Tom had always been a dog man, but the cats were growing on him. He sat next to Sam and said, "How was your afternoon?" She held up a finger and kept reading for a minute, then put the book down and looked at him.

"It's getting really good."

"I'm waiting for you to pull an all-nighter toward the end."

"I have to be careful about how close I am if I pick it up at night." She smiled.

"How was your afternoon?"

"Great. I popped in to see my friend Tia, Melissa, Randy and Edna at the hotel, and Mr. Williams at the post office. I don't see some of them very often, so it was fun catching up. Then I came home and took Ghost for a ride. Bear seems to be doing very well. I had an idea, too, but I want to wait until Jack gets back before I tell you about it."

"Why is that?"

"Because it involves a place that belongs to him."

"I didn't know he owned property up here."

"He inherited it from a woman he was dating."

"She died?"

"Yes, remember those murders I told you about? She was one of them. Jack was crushed."

"You went through a lot last year."

"The last couple of years have been traumatic. I keep waiting for things to calm down. They will, won't they? Santo Milagro is a sleepy little town where nothing more exciting than a wedding ever happens." Her brow furrowed. "At least, that's how it used to be."

"Now that I'm here, we'll probably go back to the case of the missing cow." He smiled. "Any thoughts about dinner?"

"I have some Bulgarian stew thawing. I can probably put it in a pot to heat now." The cats complained when she got up, then followed her into the kitchen to get their dinner. "We should light a fire. That would be nice this evening, don't you think?"

"Yeah. I think I can manage that. Do I need to open the flue?"

"Probably. I haven't had a fire since last winter. Holler if you need a hand. I froze the rest of the lasagna, but we have left over salad and French bread we can eat with the stew."

"I like the idea of freezing leftovers. That way, we don't get sick of anything and have something we can make easily for dinner."

"I've been doing that since my abuela died. It was just my father and me, so we could never eat a full pan of anything in one sitting."

"I'd like to hear more about your childhood sometime, and I'll tell you about mine. Fire's roaring."

"One thing I've been wanting to do since Jack first came to town is make the attic into an open third floor. I've been afraid of the attic since I was a child. I found out that it's because Jack locked me in there when I was small, but it doesn't help my irrational fear. I'd like to open it up, with stairs and lots of light."

"That sounds like a great idea. Should we make it into another bedroom? Or maybe a library?"

"Let's make it into a library with lots of windows and plants.

When we have electrical storms, we can sit up there at night and watch them."

"We should put a love seat by the windows so we can snuggle while we watch."

Sam smiled at him. "Oh! The stew. I almost burned it."

Jack walked into the kitchen and sniffed. "Smells like something good. You're turning into a regular housewife."

"Yep." She winked at Tom. "Are you hungry?"

"Famished."

"Go get cleaned up, and we'll be ready to chow."

Jack went upstairs.

Tom asked, "Does everyone always have to shower before dinner?"

"No, but Jack works with dead bodies all day." She scrunched her nose. "I figure it's best to get the dead off of him before we share a meal."

Tom laughed. "Good point. I didn't think of that. Let me help you set the table."

When Jack returned, he sat at the table and looked in his bowl. "What is this?"

"Bulgarian stew. You'll love it."

"Where did you learn how to make it?"

"I have an online friend who gave me the recipe."

"Is it quick?"

"Nope. I made it before we went camping, though, and froze the leftovers."

Jack took a bite and agreed it was delicious. "It would make a perfect au jus for roast beef sandwiches."

"It would. We'll have to try that tomorrow. Hey Jack? I had an idea today and wanted to ask you what you thought about it."

"What's that?" He continued eating.

"I was walking around, visiting friends in town, and realized that we are missing a couple of things. One is a bookstore. We don't have one. The other is a large venue for weddings and parties.

I was thinking about Alley's saloon and wondering if you might be willing to sell or lease it."

He frowned. "To whom?"

"To me."

"You want to open a bookstore and rent out the space for public functions?"

"Yeah. I was thinking about it."

"What about the survival camping?"

"I might be able to give classes at the store and have a camp once a month during moderate seasons. I don't want to put myself or anyone else through what we just went through."

"I need to think about it, okay?"

She looked at him. "Okay." Sam looked down at her food, a little disappointed in his answer. It was his property, though, so if he wanted it to sit there unused, that was his decision.

After a quiet dinner, he got up to do the dishes, but Sam pushed him away. "It's fine. I just heated it up. I'll do the dishes. Go enjoy the fire.

Chapter 22

Jack and Tom went into the living room to sit by the fire. "Is she mad at me?"

"I don't know. You know your dynamic better than I do."

"She wants me to give up something that was important to Alley for a bookstore and community meeting place?"

"I didn't know Alley, but if it was important to her, would she rather it sat empty? Sam didn't ask you to sell it. She suggested a lease."

"I don't know. I just said I would need to think about it."

"That's fair. I don't see how she can deny you that."

"She's acting like I said something wrong."

"You know how she is. She decided she wants to do something, and she doesn't like roadblocks. She'll think about it and realize she's rushing."

"Maybe. Our relationship has changed somewhat, and I don't know what she wants from me." He stood slowly with a furrowed brow. "I think I'll go up to bed. See you in the morning."

"Okay. Goodnight."

Jack went upstairs, and Tom sat lost in thought until the fire had smoldered to ashes, but Sam didn't join him.

Wandering into the kitchen and finding it empty, he went upstairs and found Sam asleep in their bed. This cousin thing is complicated. He put on his pajamas and slipped under the covers, wondering how to resolve this new hurdle.

Sam was still asleep next to him when Tom woke the next morning.

He dressed quietly and went down to the kitchen, only to find it still and odorless. Strange. He brewed a pot of coffee and made himself some toast. By eight o'clock, no one was around, so he poured himself a second cup of coffee and left for work, noticing that Jack's truck was gone.

On his drive in, he decided that he should stay out of the fray. It was not his place to interfere in cousinly warfare. They were adults and should resolve their differences on their own. If he interfered, they would just resent his intrusion. He arrived at the station at the same time as Mick, and they sat at Mick's desk to go over what they had discovered the previous day.

"Today, we should interview David," Mick said.

"I agree. If he's presented with enough evidence, it should at least encourage him to think about his options."

"He'll probably lawyer up."

"He can do that, but it won't change the outcome."

"Let's hope not. We should probably consult with the DA's office."

"Before or after we interview him?"

"Before, I think. Let's find out what we need to accomplish. I'll call him now and set up an appointment."

Tom's phone rang. "I'll take this while you make your call." He stood and walked down the hall before answering. "Hello, Sam. Good morning."

"Hi. Did you make the coffee this morning?"

"I did. Did I make it wrong?"

"No, it's perfect. Thank you. I was just checking."

"The kitchen was silent and empty when I got up, so I fended for myself."

"I'm sorry. I should have set my alarm."

"Don't feel like you have to babysit. I've taken care of myself for a long time."

"I know, but since I don't have a full-time job, I can help you out."

"Sam…"

"No, I know. I need to figure out what I'm going to do. I was traumatized by that survival camp, and I'm re-thinking my path."

"Consider that your full-time job for now. You don't have to wait on me. You're my partner, not my servant. I just want some company and some affection. Anything else isn't necessary."

"I'm going to cry now."

"No, don't do that. I love you. I need you to love me too. That's all. Let's have pizza tonight and talk about your options, okay?"

"With Modelo Negra?"

"Absolutely. I love you."

"I love you too. Thank you."

"Kiss kiss."

Both hung up smiling.

After speaking with the DA's office, Mick went looking for Tom. "Come on, slacker. We have a meeting in Las Rodillas."

They got in the cruiser and were silent for the first part of the trip.

"Is everything alright at home?" Mick finally asked.

"Yes, I guess so. Sam is having a small crisis because she's not sure if she wants to do any more survival camps, and she got into a strange, silent argument with Jack last night about the use of one of his properties."

"Uh oh. Don't get involved in that one."

"Right?" Tom blew out air from his nose.

"They'll figure it out. Just be supportive and don't offer advice."

"The thing is, I feel like if I weren't part of the equation, they wouldn't be having this disagreement."

"That might be true. But you are part of the equation, so they'll just have to work it out."

"Why does everything have to be so complicated?"

"Just be patient. Concentrate on the job. The rest will work itself out."

"I hope so."

Mick pulled up in front of an imposing brick edifice. "Come on in and meet our prosecutor."

They walked into the city offices and took the decrepit, creaking elevator to the third floor. The hallway and the elevator smelled moldy, like wet towels. Entering the prosecutor's office, Mick announced their arrival, and they sat to wait. Tom looked around the lobby, pleasantly surprised by the homey, inviting atmosphere and the fresh smell. He spied a slightly open window and an air freshener in one of the outlets.

"Mr. Travis will see you now," the receptionist informed them before leading them down a long, carpeted hallway and knocking on a solid, wooden door. She let them in, then silently disappeared on the other side of the door.

"Hello, gentlemen," Mr. Travis rose to greet them, his gleaming black hair and athletic build belying his advanced age.

"Hello, Mr. Travis. This is Detective Thomas Cork. He's recently joined us from Las Vegas."

"Las Vegas. Quite a downgrade. To what do we owe the pleasure?"

"Marital bliss, I'm afraid. My new bride is a rancher from Santo Milagro."

Mr. Travis chuckled. "Marital bliss indeed. Welcome. How are you enjoying it so far?"

"So far, so good."

"Excellent." He nodded. "Have a seat. Please. You two have an interesting case, it looks like."

Mick explained the circumstances. "It appears that the murderer attempted to frame his sister for his crime.'

"You have evidence?"

"Yes, and the testimony of his sister and their cousin. We're going to interview him now and wondered if you have any advice."

"My advice? Make sure he is offered the opportunity to consult with an attorney. Solicit as much information as you can.

Your evidence should be solid, not circumstantial. What do you have so far?"

They laid out everything they had and spoke with the lawyer at length before heading to the jail to interview David.

When David was brought into the interview room, he smiled at Tom and Mick with confidence and sat at the table. "Hi, Tom. How's your back?"

"Much better, thank you. Are you certain you don't want an attorney to represent you during our interview?"

"I'm sure. There is no reason why I should need one."

"If you change your mind at any time, you can stop the interview and request one to be present."

David shrugged. "Sure."

"Your sister, Holly, told us in her first statement that you killed her friend Scott Jacobs but referred to you as her brother rather than by your name, so we mistakenly thought she was referring to your cousin Ernie."

"Did you ask Ernie?"

"Yes, once he had woken from his coma, he agreed that it was you who killed Scott, and you told him that he should accept blame in order to protect you."

David looked surprised.

"Holly has asserted from the beginning that she had nothing to do with Art's murder, but we were presented with the evidence of the small, blood-soaked jacket and gloves, the small footprints, and your and Ernie's statements that contradicted her testimony."

David nodded.

"Forensic evidence, however, has shown that the jacket was not Holly's and that the knife couldn't have entered Art the way you said it did. Additionally, Ernie retracted his initial statement and said that you killed Art and told him to lie in order to protect you. Your appearance at the ranch, and subsequent conversation with Jack, have led us to believe that you murdered both Scott Jacobs and Art Jimenez."

"You have both lost your minds."

"Would you like to make a statement regarding these charges?"

"I would like Holly and Ernie to come in here and accuse me to my face."

"We can arrange for Holly to come in here, but Ernie, as you know, is currently in the hospital."

"Fine. I will take your offer of an attorney. Find me one and bring Holly in here to accuse me to my face."

Tom sat with David until his attorney arrived, then left them to confer while he went to speak with Holly.

The attorney, Mr. Finley, indicated that they were ready, so Tom and Mick reentered the interview room. "My client has decided not to answer any more questions."

"But I still want Holly to come in here and accuse me to my face."

"I have advised you against this."

"Bring her."

Mick went to the door and spoke with the deputy, who brought Holly in without handcuffs. She walked in and stood near Tom. "I cannot believe that you would stoop so low as to kill Art and then frame me for it. You not only took away my one true love, but then you tried to take away my freedom too. What kind of brother would do that? I thought you loved me. I thought you were looking out for me. How could you?"

David looked her in the eye. "What kind of sister would try to blame her crime on her brother? Do you think they believe you? Do you think they brought you in here to make me look bad? They are building a strong case against you. You should have trust-ed me. Look at you now. You've just proved me right."

"You're sick. I didn't really understand that until this moment. May I go now?"

"Yes. Thank you for your cooperation," Tom said.

"You're letting her go?"

"Yes. The evidence doesn't lie."

"I'll get you for this, Holly. Do you hear me? You're dead!" he yelled as she left.

"I can't help you if you don't keep your mouth shut," Mr. Finley said.

"Get out. You're useless."

Mr. Finley walked out with Tom and Mick, and the deputy took David back to his cell. Holly was in the reception area, retrieving her belongings.

"Do you need a ride somewhere?" Mick asked.

"I don't have anywhere to go. I lived with Art."

"Why don't we take you to your grandmother's house? She thinks highly of you."

"Does she? She's a funny lady."

"We were just out there yesterday. She gave us cookies."

"Okay. I'll take you up on your offer. Thank you."

When they pulled up to Mrs. Cooper's house, she ran outside with tears streaming down her face and hugged Holly. "I'm so glad you're okay. Will you be staying with me for a while?"

"If you don't mind."

"Yes, yes. You're welcome for as long as you like." She turned to Mick. "Thank you, Sergeant."

"Any time, ma'am. Just save me some cookies."

She grinned at him. "I'll be baking another batch this evening."

Mick and Tom took their leave, and Mrs. Cooper led Holly into the house.

Chapter 23

Tom got home early that evening, but he was exhausted. Sam ran him a hot bath and asked if he still wanted pizza.

"Pizza sounds perfect," he said as he climbed into the bath. Sam ordered two while he soaked. When they arrived, she left one on the table for Jack and took the other upstairs. Tom had fallen asleep in the bath, so Sam helped him get dried off and ready for bed. They ate some pizza, then went to bed early.

Sam lay quietly, watching his strong, kindly face in repose. She said her nightly prayer with gratitude, before finally drifting off into a dreamless sleep.

Although he considered staying in Las Rodillas, Jack changed his mind and drove back to the ranch. He was surprised to find an uneaten pizza on the table until he spied Sam's note: *For Jack* was all it said. He ate a couple of slices and put the rest in the fridge, then fell asleep in front of the television.

Since Sam had bought him pizza, he reciprocated by making coffee and breakfast before he left in the morning. He didn't like fighting with her and hoped it would blow over soon. He was done with the autopsies but didn't want to leave while they were on bad terms. I could just give her what she wants, but that's not a good way to solve a disagreement. *Maybe I should just leave.*

His phone rang at about ten, and it was Sam. He thought about letting it go to voicemail but answered. "Jack Olivares."

"I know that, silly." He could hear the smile in her voice. "I'm sorry I wasn't up when you got home. Tom fell asleep in the bath."

"That's okay. Thank you for the pizza."

"I'm also sorry that I made you feel bad about not letting me use the saloon. I had no right. I just don't know what to do with myself. I'll figure something out. Not every idea will be the right one."

"I didn't say no. I just asked for some time to think about it."

"I know. But I also think you're not ready to make that decision, so I'll think of something else. Captain Blatt thinks I should join the sheriff's department." She laughed.

"Maybe you should."

"I think I would have trouble with the desk work."

"You might. You're used to having a lot of autonomy."

"Yeah."

"Anyway, I'm about done here, so I'll be going back to Albuquerque tomorrow. Do you want to go out to eat or something tonight?"

"No, I'll make something. Any requests?"

"Whatever's easy. I'll be back about six."

He hung up and was filled with sadness. He had thought everything was fine, but it wasn't.

Sam hung up and sat at the kitchen table. She didn't know what was wrong, but something had changed between her and Jack. Their easy camaraderie was gone and in its place was something foreign. *I shouldn't have brought up the saloon.* She got up and went outside to see Ghost.

"Hello, Ms. Sam." Roger walked out, followed by Red and Bear, and Sam had to giggle.

"If you get one more, you'll have your own parade. Why do you suppose they're doing that? I understand Bear being clingy, but he seems to be following Red's lead at the same time, and Red is usually more independent, isn't he?"

Roger looked at the dogs and nodded. "It's curious. Red seems to understand, no? I'm proud of him. Are you wanting to go for a ride?"

"Yes, I need some Ghost time." She smiled.

"Want some company?"

Sam sighed. "No… yes… I don't know. I'm feeling a little lost right now. You usually have some good advice."

"I'll come along if you don't mind. The dogs can get some exercise, and I'll be quiet if you just want to think."

He brought Ghost out, and Sam talked to her and hugged her while he saddled up his own horse. When he was ready, Sam leaped onto Ghost, and they walked out into the paddock. She stared unseeing at the dogs racing around the open space and tried to untangle her snarled thoughts. Roger startled her when he said, "Do you want to talk about what's bothering you?"

"I feel like I felt before I left for Las Vegas, and it frightens me." Pausing, her mouth turned down. "I should be filled with gratitude and bliss, but I seem to have come full circle. I don't think I've grown or changed at all."

"How did you feel when you left for Vegas?"

"I felt upset about Jack, and I was lonely and bored."

"Have you talked to Tom about this?"

She shook her head. "I'm afraid he might be insulted or feel like I don't love him."

"What happened with Jack?"

"I don't know. We were so close, and then he left."

"He came here when you were gone." He leaned over to open the gate that led to the river, and they walked their horses through.

"I know. We talked about that up on the mountain, and everything seemed okay. Then I asked him about using the saloon for a project, and we ended up not speaking until I apologized. He's leaving tomorrow, and there's something wrong between us."

"When he was here before, it was just you and him against the world. Now, it's you and Tom. It's a big adjustment, no?"

"It was just the two of us until he met Alley and then again after she died. I was okay with their relationship."

"But it was your house, and she didn't move in with you."

"True."

"Do you regret marrying Tom?"

Sam paused and thought about Tom. "No, I love Tom, but I feel kind of disconnected right now and resentful that he's come between Jack and me. He hasn't done it on purpose. I thought they might become great friends at one point."

The rushing water of the river tumbled and roared, and they stopped the horses near the shore, silently absorbing the negative ions suffusing the air.

"Would you like my advice?" Roger asked quietly.

Sam nodded.

"I think you should plan another camp once the trial is over, maybe just with friends. We can go up there and do it the way you planned. Then, you can decide if you want to keep doing it or if you want to do something else. You know what they say about falling off a horse, huh."

She looked at him and let out a deep breath. "Losing Art when he was trying to protect me… seeing Tom shot… being alone in the cold, and afraid for my life… sometimes I wake up drenched in sweat with my heart pounding."

"You need a do-over. Camping and hiking are important to you. You don't want one bad experience to take them away."

She shivered.

"Talk to Tom about it and plan another. The rest of us will rally around you."

"Perhaps. After the trial. I'll pray about it." She looked around. "We're at the place where we had our picnic."

Roger smiled. "It seems like a good place to hash out our problems."

"My problems, mostly. Thanks, Roger."

"Ready to head back?"

"Yes. My head's a little clearer now."

"Good." He whistled for the dogs, and they headed back to the ranch.

With a heavy heart, Sam prepared Jack's farewell dinner. She knew that they needed time to adjust but the transition was painful. Tom got home at five and showered before joining her in the kitchen. He sat at the table and watched her cook.

"Any news about the case?" she asked.

"Yes, David finally confessed. He admitted to shooting me, killing Scott, killing Art, and framing Holly."

"What made him decide to do that?"

"When we laid out all of the evidence and the two witnesses, his lawyer told him he was going to be convicted and that he might have the possibility of parole if he plead guilty."

"Will he get parole?"

"I'd say it's highly unlikely."

Sam kept working on the enchiladas.

"I've noticed you seem unhappy, Sam. Is it because of me?"

She kept her back to him and shook her head, unable to speak. Tears glistened in her eyes when he approached, turning her around to face him, so he hugged her silently as the tears fell.

Once Sam had composed herself, she pulled away, gave Tom a kiss, and splashed some water on her face. She looked at him and swallowed. "Tonight is Jack's last night with us, and I've invited a few people for dinner. Can you help me set the table?"

"Sure. We'll talk later?"

Sam pressed her lips in a line and nodded.

"It's not something I've done?"

"No, you're the one great thing I've got going for me."

He brushed his fingers along her sleeve, and his lips turned up slightly as he moved toward the silverware drawer.

The guests trickled into the kitchen—Roger and Melissa, Ben, Mick, then Jorge, Jack's favorite people in Santo Milagro. Everyone sat at the table and accepted a beer. The clock chimed six, then seven, but Jack didn't show up. Finally, Tom went into the living room and called him, but he didn't answer.

Tom texted, "Sam made enchiladas. Five guests are sitting at the kitchen table, and we have been waiting to eat. Could you let us know if we should go ahead?"

He received an answer five minutes later. "I have returned to Albuquerque. Please thank Sam for me." Tom stared at his phone and cringed. He walked back into the kitchen. "Jack has been detained and said to go ahead without him. I'm sorry, Sam, but we have great company, and the enchiladas smell delicious."

Everyone was still for a moment until Jorge, who didn't know any better, broke the tension. "Enchilada party. Woo!"

Everyone joined in and helped to make the atmosphere festive.

Sam served the enchiladas with beans and rice and an ice cream cake for dessert. She enjoyed the meal with her friends, but inside she was grieving.

Chapter 24

*H*angovers are the worst. Sam held her head. She drank more than she should have the night before and fell asleep before she could talk to Tom. Brushing her teeth and getting dressed before gingerly heading down the stairs she smelled the bacon first, then coffee. She entered the kitchen to discover her wonderful husband sitting at the table reading her book. She looked at the clock in confusion. "Shouldn't you be at work?"

He looked up and smiled. "Good morning, beautiful. I called in today."

"Why? Aren't you feeling well?"

"I got the job so I could be with you, and I'm pretty sure you need to talk to me."

"Oh, Tom. I'm such a mess, and I don't know what I did to deserve you." She wrapped her arms around his shoulders and rubbed her head against his like a cat.

"Get yourself a cup of coffee and some breakfast. We have all the time in the world." He smiled again.

She sat at the table with him and began to feel better once she had something in her stomach.

"I think I might have an inkling of what you've been going through, but I'd like you to tell me if you can."

Sam gazed into his kind, blue eyes and almost broke down again. "I don't know where to start. So many terrible things have happened."

"Why don't we start with macro and work our way to micro. What are the big-picture events?"

Sam thought about that. "My dream of pursuing my passion and my relationship with Jack are in shambles. I feel almost like I did when I left for Las Vegas."

"What's different?"

"You're here with me."

"Which one do you want to talk about first?"

"You helped me find my passion. I was so busy and excited during my training and while I was planning the camp. I had images in my head of happy campers, lively meals together, tromping around in the woods, learning, but then everything went wrong."

"It did. Was any of it your fault? Could you have prevented it?"

"No, I don't think so."

"Is it likely to happen again?"

She shook her head. "But the things that happened changed me."

"How?"

"I've never been afraid in the woods, even by myself. I've always believed that I could take care of myself."

"You did take care of yourself."

"But I couldn't keep you safe, or Scott, or Art."

"I'm a detective. I investigate homicides. That's what I do. What do you suppose would happen if I blamed myself for not preventing them?"

Sam looked at him.

"It would destroy me, Sam. No one can assume that type of responsibility. A determined killer will be successful. The best we can do is make sure he's behind bars, so he doesn't kill again."

"But Art was a big part of my dream. He trained me and helped me set up my business. He was my mentor and my friend. Now he's gone." Sam's tears leaked from her eyes, and she blinked them back.

"He was part of the dream but not the reason you pursued it."

"And the time I spent in the shelter and the cave. I hated that. What kind of survival trainer hates primitive survival?"

"Survival isn't always fun, but the point is that you knew what to do in an emergency. If you hadn't had that training, you might have frozen to death. Teaching others how to take care of themselves in an emergency situation might save a life one day."

Sam got up to get another cup of coffee. "Do you want some?" She held up the pot.

"Sure. I'll have one more."

She poured him a cup and sat back down. "I guess you're right. My dream didn't die; I just couldn't see past the trauma. Roger told me I should try again. Maybe a small camp or just with friends."

"That sounds like a good idea." He took her hand. "Now, tell me about Jack."

Her eyes and her mouth tilted downward, and she shook her head. "I don't know what happened. Everything seemed okay until I mentioned the saloon. He seemed to just shut down. I even called him and apologized and told him I'd make dinner for him last night. Our relationship is broken, and I don't know how to fix it."

"Maybe he just needs time."

"He doesn't operate that way. He'll just bury his feelings with a mountain of work. This was the first time I'd seen him or even really had a conversation with him since before I went to Las Vegas. I thought things were back to normal after we talked about what happened." She hunched over and stared into her empty cup.

"I'm sorry, Sam. I know how important he is to you."

She felt her anxiety well up inside her and had to concentrate on her breathing. "I need to go outside for a while," she said before rising from the table and grabbing her coat on the way to the door.

Tom remained at the table, thinking about Sam and Jack, wondering if there was any-thing he could do to help. *It's my fault they're at odds. She married me before they had a chance to work out their problems.* He sat there a long time, waiting for her to return, but she didn't, so he got up and washed the dishes, then went to work.

When he got to the station, Mick was sitting at his desk doing paperwork. He looked up and said, "Good to see you. Everything okay at the ranch?"

"Sort of. Aftermath of the Jack debacle."

Mick gazed at him and nodded. "Here's some paperwork to keep you busy." He handed Tom a stack of folders.

"Ah, the fun part of the job. Have you heard from the prosecutor?"

"Yes, the hearing is the day after tomorrow. He's not expecting it to go to trial, but if it does, he's prepared."

Sam rode Ghost for a long time, not paying much attention to where they were. She was jolted from her reverie by a familiar voice. "Hey, Sam. What are you doing way out here?" Holly was in the front yard of a neat, little house, sweeping the last of the snow from the walkway.

"Hi. I didn't know you lived out here."

"I didn't. I lived with Art. This is my gran's house. Would you like to come in? She makes the best bizcochitos."

"Yes, thank you." She told Ghost to wait for her and went inside.

"We can have tea on the porch if you want to watch your horse."

"That might be best. If she wanders off, I won't have a ride home." Sam smiled.

"Come meet Gran anyway, then we can sit outside."

The house felt cozy and old-fashioned, with warm colors and comfortable furniture. "Gran!" Holly called. "There's someone I'd like you to meet."

Sam recognized the petite elderly woman from town. "Hello, Mrs. Cooper. I didn't realize Holly was your granddaughter."

"Hello, Sam. It's lovely to see you. How did you two meet?"

"She was running the survival camp I was telling you about."

"Such a small world." Mrs. Cooper's tinkling laugh was infectious, and Sam smiled.

"Could we have some tea and cookies on the porch? Sam's horse is out there, and she wants to keep an eye on her."

"Of course, dear. Go and get comfortable, and I'll bring it right out."

Holly gave her a hug and thanked her before leading Sam back out front. "I didn't know where to go when they released me, so Mick brought me here. Sit anywhere." She indicated a cluster of wicker furniture and a swing.

"You seem different than when you were at camp."

"I was angry at you and at Art and caught up in David's machinations, then I started losing people I cared about. I was still angry but then frightened and gutted when Art died. I didn't know who to trust. I still don't know what I'll do without Art. My entire world was wrapped up in him."

Sam studied her downturned, bloodshot eyes as she blinked back her tears. "I have a proposition for you."

Mrs. Cooper came out just then, so Holly jumped up to help her with the tray. "Thanks, Gran." She returned to her seat, setting the tray down and pouring tea for them both before asking, "What's your proposition?"

"I've discovered that I don't like being in the woods alone, eating survival food, and if I'm truthful, I'm a little afraid after what happened. You told me that your survival camps were more hardcore. I was wondering if you might like to join forces. Art told me you're really good, maybe as good as he was."

Holly's lips tilted up when Sam said that. "We liked to challenge each other."

"Well, since you lost your partner and I lost my chutzpah, I thought perhaps we could run our camps together."

Holly gazed at Sam. "You trust me after everything that happened?"

"Are you angry at me for anything else?"

"No, you've been the one person who's been in my corner, even after I hit you on the head with a rock. At this point, I trust you with my life."

"Would you be angry if I told you Art left me everything?"

Holly gaped at her. "He did?"

"That's what the lawyer said, but I don't know if he left me a note or instructions or anything."

"He didn't know if he could trust me. It makes me sad but not angry. You were a good friend to him."

"Once it gets through probate, I intend to give the house back to you, and if we're partners, you'll have the business as well. I'd like to keep Bear, though. He's happy where he is."

"Oh, Sam. That would make me so happy." Holly began crying in earnest and ended up with hiccups.

"The house isn't contingent on your partnership. It's yours either way. But if you want to try it out, I would like that."

"Can I visit Bear sometime?"

"Sure. Do you know where I live?"

"Yes. David pointed it out on the way to camp."

Sam shivered.

"I know how you feel. There's something wrong with him. I just didn't realize it for a long time. I thought Art was overreacting. I wish I had listened."

Sam finished her tea and stood. "Stop by whenever you like, to see Bear or just to visit. When you're ready, we can talk about the survival camp."

Holly stood too and hugged Sam around her waist since Sam was nine inches taller. "I'll see you soon." She waved as Sam mounted Ghost and headed for home.

Chapter 25

Handing Ghost off to Roger, Sam raced for the house, excited to tell Tom about her conversation with Holly. She ran into the kitchen and found it clean and empty. Both cats were staring at her with their imperious 'feed us' looks. She ran upstairs and found some of Tom's clothes missing. His toothbrush and razor were gone from the bathroom. Sam sat on the bed, puzzled. *Did he have to go on a trip? Maybe he left a note.* She walked back downstairs to look. No note. She called Mick.

"Hi Mick, do you know where Tom's gone?"

There was silence on the other end of the line. "I'm not sure. He was here, then he said he needed a leave of absence, and he left. I'm pretty sure that's a record."

"Did he say anything about where he was going?"

"When he came in this afternoon, he was worrying about having come between you and Jack. He blamed himself."

"Oh, no. Thanks, Mick."

Sam hung up and went back outside. Tom's bike was gone. "Roger," she called, "Did Tom say anything to you before he left?"

"All he said was, 'Tell Sam I'm sorry.'"

Sam's heart was pounding, and she was sucking in air. "I don't even know where to look for him."

"Come on inside. You look white as a sheet." Roger helped her get seated at the table and heated a cup of coffee for her. "Why don't you try texting him and see if he responds. If he doesn't, we can try calling friends and relatives."

She sipped her coffee. *Would he have gone to talk to Jack without telling me?*

195

She pulled out her phone and sent him a text message. *Tom, I got home all excited to tell you about my visit with Holly, but you are gone without even a note. Are you okay? Did you decide I'm too much trouble? I meant it when I said you were the only good thing in my life. Please don't leave me. I love you. Sam*

Tom pulled his Harley into the hotel parking lot and looked up at the three-story orange and tan building. He removed his saddlebags and glanced at his phone. Reading Sam's message, his heart sank. Of course, she'd assume that I was leaving her. What else would she think? I should have left a note. He had left in a hurry and didn't want her to try to stop him from talking to Jack. The two of them were both stubborn and had trouble communicating sometimes. Tom wanted to try to get the ball rolling. He checked into his hotel, sent Sam a quick text assuring her he would be back soon and drove to the University of New Mexico, where Jack's office was located.

When Jack walked into the lobby and saw Tom, his expression remained motionless, except for one raised eyebrow. "Tom, what a surprise. How can I help you?"

"Could we speak in private?"

"Of course. Come on back to my office." He ushered Tom inside and indicated a chair. "Did Sam send you?" he asked as he closed the door.

"No. She doesn't know I'm here."

The eyebrow rose again. "How did you manage that?"

"I left while she was out."

Jack rubbed his eyes. "What do you want, Tom?"

Tom hung his head. "She's so unhappy. She said she feels like she did before she left for Las Vegas. I'm worried about her. Is there anything I can do to help?"

"No. You'll have to leave this one alone."

"Can you tell me what happened?"

"I don't even know. Something." Jack shrugged. "Maybe I'll let you know once I figure it out."

"It's my fault, isn't it. I didn't realize."

"Would it have stopped you?"

"I don't know. Maybe. If I had realized the consequences.

"You could always divorce her and leave me to pick up the pieces."

Tom thought he was joking until he looked into his eyes. There in the deep, black depths, he realized that Jack was at least partially serious. "Do you think that would make her happier?"

"Ha. You're asking me that? After you told me you couldn't live without her?"

"I don't know if I can, but it tears me up seeing her so unhappy."

"Go home, Tom. She'll cope. She's very resilient. Let me deal with my own demons."

"As you wish. Let me know if you want anything from me."

"Just make her happy. That's all."

Tom left Jack's office, checked out of his hotel, and drove home.

Sitting in the turkey coop with Antoine, Sam's head jerked up when Tom drove into the yard. She sprung to her feet and ran to meet him. Throwing her arms around him almost before he got off his bike, she hugged him hard. "I thought you left me," she cried.

He hugged her back and smoothed her hair. "I will never leave you, Sam. I love you more than life itself."

"Where did you go?"

"I tried to interfere because I couldn't stand to see you so unhappy."

She gazed into his eyes uncomprehendingly.

"I went to see Jack. I didn't want you to try to stop me."

"You are a wonderful husband. It didn't help, did it."

"Yes and no. It didn't help you and Jack, but it helped me understand a little bit better."

"Understand what?"

"Your dynamic, I guess. Jack, maybe. Both of you run away when you get overwhelmed, I think. Is that true?"

"Yes, but I'm not going to run away anymore because I trust you."

"You didn't trust me this morning."

"But now I do. Just don't ever leave with your toothbrush and forget to write a note.

"It will never happen again."

They were distracted by frantic gobbling and a giant, cowering ball of fur.

"Oh no! Antoine." Sam went running for the coop and almost collided with Roger. She scooped up the turkey, and he hugged Bear. "I guess we should introduce them properly, so they don't frighten each other to death."

Roger stroked Bear and talked to him gently as Sam knelt with Antoine. Both calmed down, and Bear gave the bird a sniff before Roger got up and called him. He gave one last look at Antoine before joining Roger with a wag of his tail. Sam gave Antoine a treat and closed up his coop.

"That could have been very ugly," she told Tom.

"Yes, Antoine got lucky that time." They smiled together and headed indoors.

Alice Kanaka has been reading everything she could get her hands on since she could hold a book and writing stories about the world around her. Her youth was a series of moves across the United States, accompanied by her sibling sidekick and her books.

After studying abroad in England and Spain and a short stint working for Club Med, Alice packed her bag once more and went to teach in Japan. Her story continues along the same vein, adding languages, kids and cats into the mix. Open one of her mysteries to see the world through her eyes. You won't be disappointed.

HTTPS://AliceKanaka.com

If you'd like to see more of Alice's adventures, make sure to check out her **travel blog!**

https://ExploringWithAlice.com

Sign up for Alice's mailing list to get discounts, notifications and exclusive short stories.

Coming Soon:
Bumfuzzle and Cattywampus,
Unlikely Detectives